Slow Lightning

Slow Lightning

A novel by
MARK FRUTKIN

RAINCOAST BOOKS
Vancouver

Raincoast Books acknowledges the ongoing support of The Canada Council; the British Columbia Ministry of Small Business, Tourism and Culture through the B.C. Arts Council; and the Government of Canada through the Book Publishing Industry Development Program (BPIDP).

First published in 2001 by

Raincoast Books

9050 Shaughnessy Street
Vancouver, B.C.
V6P 6E5
(604) 323-7100

www.raincoast.com

Edited by Joy Gugeler
Typeset by Bruce Collins
Cover photo by Marie-Louise Brimberg/Firstlight
Cover design by Les Smith

1 2 3 4 5 6 7 8 9 10

CANADIAN CATALOGUING IN PUBLICATION DATA

National Library of Canada Cataloguing in Publication Data

Frutkin, Mark, 1948-

  Slow lightning

ISBN 1-55192-406-4

I. Title.
PS8561.R84S56 2001   C813'.54   C2001-910226-7
PR9199.3.F776S56 2001

Printed and bound in Canada

For Elliot, because he asked

*Like lightning it begins and ends
in the same moment.*
— Cervantes, on love

*...the truth I wished for came
cleaving my mind in a great flash of light.*
— Dante, *Paradiso*

Contents

Barcelona 1

The Saint James Way 33

The Cave at Arcasella 127

A Man in Flames 173

Entering the cave, I walk through the twisting limestone passageways, deeper and deeper into the guts of the earth, back to its primordial memory, back into the silence that existed before anything else.

I see overhead, upside-down gardens of gypsum needles. I pass pisoliths, cave pearls and mineral flowers blossoming out of uneven walls, curtains of flowstone like ghosts frozen in mid-waver, orchids of calcium carbonate, pale, as in a light-starved forest. I step around encrusted gours, pools of icy, clear water without reflection.

Entering the last gallery, I feel the deep heartbeat of the Earth within me. This, I know, is where it all begins. This the rare space from which everything is borne forth. I go inside, hunt light in the core of darkness.

§

The cave was a typical Franco-Cantabrian tunnel, running deep into limestone beneath a mountain dark with pines. Like the alleys of an Arabian souk, the caverns twisted and splayed, offered up dead ends and false passageways, turned and led into nothingness. Sandro's oil lamp, pulsing with ambiguous light, slipped along the walls. Forests of stalagmites mirrored stalactites, an architecture of strange balanced columns.

At a split he took the left tunnel, stepped across a trickle of black water, ascended a slope of loose gravel. One more turn and he would be there.

The perfection of this final gallery always took his breath away. Like an intimate medieval church, its cove ceilings sloped to stone walls.

His light penetrated every corner. He could see his bedding near the back, painting supplies piled on two flat rocks, foodstuffs on one end of a wooden crate that doubled as a table. Half a dozen books were stacked on the left.

A bestiary of life-size Paleolithic animals circled him: wild Camargue horses, bulls, bison, a small prancing ibex, aurochs, deer. He turned, swept his lamp over them. On the wall behind his bedding, he made note of where he would paint the next bull. Instantly, the power and energy of the beast rose within him. He was ready to begin.

Barcelona

April 1936

The reflection of the sun caught in the store window wavered with heat as Sandro turned to look at his other self in the dark glass: *I who despise lies am about to embark on a life that is nothing but a lie.*

He turned again and glanced back the way he had come. Workers, gentlemen, students, housewives and soldiers streamed by in both directions. No one paid him any mind. It would be a most inopportune moment to meet any acquaintances. How would he explain where he was headed?

And what if I am discovered? What then? No, this is madness.

As he continued along the street, a string bag hanging from his left hand, spring sunshine burning on the back of his neck, he tried to appear nonchalant. He failed utterly. A trickle of sweat wormed under his collar.

Entering the Ramblas, the wide street overarched with plane trees, he was glad of the sprinkling of shade. From a bird-seller's stall, caged finches and parakeets chirped at passersby.

Approaching a newsvendor's rack, he noticed a rightist paper with a photo of the spectacled face of Emilio Mola, looking more like an accountant than a general. From another stared a blurred image of Largo Caballero, the socialist leader known as the Spanish Lenin. A third carried a photo of a crowd of right-wing Falangists at a funeral, the headline shouting: SPAIN! ONE, GREAT and FREE!

Next to the newspaper, he spotted a magazine, the head of a bull on its cover. Sandro stared at it, as if caught in a trance. He followed the sweep of horns with his eyes. The bull's massive head was bowed, its snout moist, its eye a black hole.

In the fishnet bag swung not an anarchist's bomb but an artist's sketchbook. Fingering the coins in his pocket with his right hand, he sat down on a bench, removed the coins and counted them. He knew how many there were, but could not resist the urge to check again. He looked about to see if anyone was watching. Replacing the coins, he took the sketchbook from the bag and opened it to the back page where he read the list he had written that morning: *hematite, manganese dioxide, red ochre, yellow ochre* . . . His lips moved silently. Nearby, the captured finches chirped as they had on every other day; Sandro found this reassuring.

§

In the shop, mahogany shelves stood floor to ceiling stacked with high-shouldered jars of dark glass, contents labeled in a precise and elegant hand. Where appropriate, the chemist had included the common name as well as the chemical appellation, each label affixed to its jar at a point exactly five centimetres beneath the lid. When Sandro had entered to the tinkle of a silver bell, the chemist, dressed in a white smock from shoulder to ankle, had stood at attention behind the counter. Sandro was glad to see there were no other customers. The chemist, who had tightly curled, heavily oiled hair, listened in silence, hands resting on the edge of the counter, as Sandro explained his needs, holding the sketchbook open so as to refer to it.

"*Por favor*, if I may consult the list from which you have been reading." The chemist held out his hand.

Sandro gave it up with slight hesitation. He passed on the black book and stepped back, as if the entire scheme, his strange fate, was now out of his hands. He hoped the chemist would not ask what use he planned to make of such an odd list of powdered minerals. Sandro glanced at the window and saw in large block letters OXIGENO PURO on the left side and ANALISES DE ORINAS on the right.

"You are a *pintor*, no?"

Sandro nodded his head gravely. "Yes, of sorts."

"If this bull's head I see drawn here is any indication, you are certainly an excellent draftsman. In any case, it is none of my business and I beg your forgiveness for my unreasonable curiosity." He returned to the list in the book. "I have the manganese dioxide, as well as the hematite. The limonite I can get for you. The red ochre, as well as the yellow, you could likely obtain at an artist's shop. *Sí, sí,* I am sure of it." He closed the sketchbook, handed it back to Sandro and went in search of supplies.

A short while later, Sandro was walking back up the Ramblas, string bag swinging from his hand, the future of his home village of Arcasella wrapped tightly in packets of brown paper.

§

Jorge gestured broadly over the emptied plates, his bulging eyes intense. "On this side you have the Right: Carlists, Falangists, capitalists, the bourgeois, the big landowners and the church. And, over here, on the Left, you have anarchists, communists, the syndicalists and trade unions, republicans, workers, farm labourers and a few poor *estudiantes*."

"And which are you?"

"You know what I am! I am a true communist. Yes, definitely. I have been involved in some 'actions' of late." Jorge looked over his shoulder to make sure the landlady could not hear them.

"What have you done?"

"Oh, not much. Passed out some illegal flyers, delivered a box of ammunition to a trade union office."

"Oh?"

"But I would do more. Much more. I believe the capitalists have had their day. We need to knock off their fine hats. Don't you think?"

"I don't know." Sandro was confused. The previous spring, at the technical school where he studied engineering, a few of the students — the poorer ones — had begun to form political factions. When a mildly reformist government had been in power, from 1931 to 1934, the clergy, landowners and military were up in arms. When a conservative government was elected, they reversed all the reforms. Everyone on the Left was incensed. When, in February 1936, a leftist Popular Front was elected, both Right and Left lost their heads entirely. The centre hardly existed. Any sense of compromise disappeared, as the Right feared a Soviet-style revolution and the Left incited crowds of workers to exercise their power. Now, in the cafés, he felt everyone's pull, and still he had no strong convictions one way or the other. He was so deeply lodged in the centre no one could hear him.

He could not keep all the groups straight. He thought Jorge had mentioned the leftist *Partido Obrero de Unificación Marxista*, or POUM as it was commonly known. Then there was the UGT, which he thought stood for the *Unión General de Trabajadores*, and there was a Socialist Party for Catalonia and the *Confederación Nacional de Trabajo* and the *Federación Anarquista Ibérica* and the *Juventud de Acción Popular*, as well as the UME and UMRA and JCI and many others. And what did it all mean? Anarchist Doctrinal Vanguard, *Juntas de Ofensiva Nacional-Sindicalista*, *Juventudes Socialistas Unificadas*. The cafés of Barcelona were exploding with intellectuals declaiming the new world or the importance of a glorious Spanish past, one party taking over each café, one party for each village, from Extremadura to Andalusia, from Asturias to Aragon.

"I will take you to some meetings." Jorge smiled. "You will get a true political education. When the *Revolución* comes, you want to be ready."

"Ready for what?" Sandro shrugged. He liked Jorge, this small ugly Catalan with his bulging eyes, heavy eyebrows, pointy face and ungainly hands.

"Ready for 'it'."

"What's 'it'?"

"The moment the workers take over the world."

"What happens to everybody else?"

"They must work, too."

"Like now."

"Well, no. The priests will have to till the fields."

"But priests don't know how to till fields; they know how to light candles and hear confessions and say Mass."

"They'll have to learn."

"And while they're learning, the rest of us will starve."

"*No importa*. Everyone will share in the difficult times. We will create a paradise on Earth."

At that moment, their landlady, Señora Garcia, walked into the room. Although a heavyset woman, she moved lightly and quietly. Jorge and Sandro stopped talking. She showed entirely too much interest.

§

Sandro eyed the yellow beer in the glass the waitress had just set down. Across the table, Jorge lifted his own and downed half of it, leaving on his upper lip a white moustache of foam he slicked away with his tongue.

"Ah, here they are."

Sandro followed Jorge's gaze toward the door. Two of their friends entered the café, a young woman with them. Sandro's breath caught in his throat.

"Who is that?"

"I believe her name is Teresa. I met her once before. The rumours say she's involved in gun smuggling, but I doubt they are true. Rumours are rampant these days." Jorge motioned them over.

The woman followed, independent of the two young men in front of her. Sandro watched her walk toward them. She moved lightly, but was unhurried. As she walked, she took in the entire room through her pores.

They exchanged greetings. The young woman neither smiled nor frowned, but, intent, regarded everything with penetrating eyes. When she was introduced to Sandro, they nodded to each other. Her medium-length black hair fell partly across her face, shading one eye.

Suddenly Sandro was aware of every sound in the room: the jumble of voices, snatches of argument, clink of glasses, scraping of chairs; as if clear radio reception had just replaced a haze of static.

The new arrivals pulled up chairs and ordered beer. Jorge spoke with Jaime and Federico about an upcoming anarchist meeting. They nodded and commented, but Teresa, like Sandro, said nothing, although she followed the conversation closely, hanging on every word.

Finally, she spoke. It was simple and profound, but something the others had clearly missed. They nodded their heads in agreement, then resumed their arguments in earnest.

Sandro watched her as she watched them. She knew he was staring, but did not discourage him. He tried to read her face, her eyes under dark eyebrows focused on Jorge as he made a point. When she reached for her glass, he noticed her hands. Not quite as rough as the hands of a peasant and yet they were marked by experience and strength. She glanced at Sandro and he lowered his gaze.

Sandro saw her three more times in the same café in the next week. Each time they nodded to each other in greeting, but never spoke. He imagined she was pleased to see him, but could not be sure.

§

Inside the entrance to the great hall, under the black flag of the anarchists, a poster read:

DOWN WITH BOURGEOIS VALUES!
NO MORE TIPPING
NO MORE BROTHELS
NO MORE CINEMAS
NO MORE DANCE HALLS
NO MORE COFFEE-DRINKING
NO MORE FANCY HAMS
NO MORE TIES
ABOVE ALL, AND MOST IMPORTANTLY,
NO MORE HATS!
THE REVOLUTION IS THE GREAT APHRODISIAC!

"Hats?" Sandro turned to Jorge, who shrugged. They went to find seats in the echoing hall that was quickly filling with workers and other students.

Anarchist and communist flags swayed like seaweed above the crowd. The cavernous space buzzed with conversation and excitement.

Jorge had insisted Sandro come with him, though he needed little encouragement. Jorge falsely assumed his friend was starting to show a genuine interest in politics. The two friends had had numerous all-night conversations about philosophy and politics in recent months. There was no doubt in Jorge's mind — the Revolution was coming, likely sooner than later.

"*Hola!* Rat Face!" a worker shouted from across the hall and waved at them. "Rat Face" was Jorge's nickname, a tag that perfectly suited his unfortunate physiognomy. Despite this, he was well liked and even garnered a certain respect for his tireless enthusiasm. Jorge may have been as ugly as a flayed rabbit, but he was known about the university for his original, strange and at times alarming way with words. Once, he had stunned his companions by comparing Spain's relationship to Europe to that of "a man with a fancy cane in a city with no cafés."

The speeches began, each speaker prophesying a new Spain, a new Catalonia. All underlined the urgency of the times — the Revolution was coming.

Those who wanted to speak simply stood up and declaimed. If the crowd disagreed, the speaker was shouted down; if they agreed, they applauded, shouted their approval and stamped their feet.

Then the hatters arrived.

The Hatters' Union entered late in the proceedings; speculators surmised that they had been plotting. A group of about thirty men, wearing hats or caps of various sorts and sizes, pushed through a side door near the stage. Their spokesman, a huge man with a long drooping handlebar moustache, his capacious cap on his head, stepped forward and, in a booming voice, addressed the clean-shaven communist hothead at the lectern.

"We demand to know why hats will be banned by the Revolution."

The young communist replied, stressing each syllable with a short, sharp downward gesture of his right hand: "Because they are a symbol of capitalism and bourgeois values."

"Will all hats be banned? What about the hat of the worker?"

"All hats must be banned, *amigo*. We must all make sacrifices for the Revolution. The Hatters' Union is no exception."

"Bah!" The spokesman waved his hairy hands about, his voice rising. "Are the pickers in the vineyards to be at the mercy of the sun?"

"Hear, hear!" his compatriots shouted.

"Are the sweepers to be at the mercy of the rain? *Qué va!* Are the mountain shepherds to bare their heads to the ice and snow?"

The young man at the lectern spoke to the assembly. "It has been agreed by the leadership. Off with your hats, my friends! We will bring in the Revolution together!" He raised his arms in the air and inspired an exultant shout from the crowd. "Think of it, friends," he shouted, the approbation of the crowd splendidly lifting his confidence. "Priests wear hats. Generals wear hats. Businessmen wear hats. We must knock those hats from their heads and trample them in the mud. Only then will the people be free of their chains." The crowd roared and rose to their feet, stamping and applauding.

When they had quieted, the spokesman for the hatters stepped forward again. "It is our livelihood," he shouted in a gravelly voice. "Are there not good hats and bad hats? Are we to ban the lowly cap along with the expensive fedora? Have you lost your minds?"

The speaker at the lectern answered. "Too many distinctions, comrade, will lead to endless discussion. Which hats to ban, which to allow, this man wants his rain hat, that man wants his sun hat. It will go on forever. Bare your heads, comrades, the Revolution is coming!"

The crowd was up and shouting again, the great hall echoing with slogans and cries of *"Viva la Revolución! Viva!"*

The hatters' spokesman stepped forward again. "If that is the workers' decision, then we shit on your *Revolución*." At that he removed his cap, as did each of his fellow union members, only to release a bird — a pigeon or starling or blackbird — that instantly shot into the air.

The birds must have been fed a laxative with their grain, for they all shit in the excitement of release. The members of the crowd shielded their heads with their arms and fled, tumbling out into the street.

§

As Sandro and Jorge trudged home through windswept streets, they continued to talk. Sandro rubbed at a white patch on his shoulder with his handkerchief. "I don't know. Perhaps the hatters have a point."

"Are you a bourgeois capitalist, then?"

"I wouldn't say that. I don't know *what* I am. I *do* know this, though — there are too many opinions. Look at what the *Revolución* is leading to — discussions about the most ridiculous things: should we wear hats or not? If so, which hats are to be forbidden? Should we allow chocolate or coffee? Should we ban the cinema? It's positively Jesuitical."

"But these things *must* be discussed. We must all pull together."

"Only those with a fanatical love of theory can look beyond their next meal. These discussions are nonsense, a waste of time."

"You *are* a capitalist."

"No, I'm not."

"An anarchist, then. You must be an anarchist."

"Why do I have to be anything? I don't believe in politics. I believe in personal choice."

"You approve of capitalists exploiting workers and peasants? You approve of the tyranny of the church? You approve of the generals sweeping in to seize power? You approve of the dead hand of tradition and privilege? You approve?"

"I approve nothing. I damn nothing. I listened to the speakers tonight. I was looking for answers. I found none."

"You cannot ignore the great struggle and pretend it does not concern you."

"No, no, the great struggle, as you call it, concerns me very much. But the great struggle is composed of many smaller struggles. It is only a Great Struggle in your mind. Don't you see?"

They stopped under a row of plane trees along the boulevard near the university. Jorge pulled a bent cigarette from his pocket, lit it and passed it to Sandro in the cool darkness.

Sandro, silent, stared at dark patches on the tree bark.

"Sandro, it is *not* a game. It is all that matters. You cannot simply run away and hide in a cave in the mountains."

"When I was in the cave the world seemed fleeting, so much dust, so many flashes of light on the wall. In the end, it is the same with all of this."

"*Muy filosófico,* my friend. But the world must change. Too many are suffering. Too many are without dignity. It is not just."

Sandro took a drag and exhaled. The city sky held few stars. "I don't know. I am not prepared to say what is just. My father is poor and uneducated and yet is the most dignified man I have ever known."

"But there is nothing noble about starvation."

"True. Still, the *Revolución* is not for me, Jorge. I refuse to make a choice."

"If you cannot make a choice, Sandro, then you had better head back to your *cueva*."

§

Sandro recalled the caves near the village of Linares in the Pyrenees where he had worked with Jorge the previous summer.

Professor Gomez had inquired at the *Politécnica* about hiring two students skilled at drafting. He wanted them to work through the summer, copying the art on the walls of a Paleolithic cave that had been discovered three years earlier by a shepherd.

Sandro remembered with fondness the many days he had spent there, lying on a blanket on the cave floor, sketching horses, bulls, bison and ibexes in a notebook, imagining the artists who had created the images twenty thousand years before. The paintings were incomparable, more beautiful, he thought, than anything he had seen hanging in the churches of Barcelona. The animals seemed alive: their thick black coats, swirling breath, quick feet and clear, innocent eyes. How had the artists rendered them so convincingly? How could his sketches do their vision justice?

Slowly, as he lay in the dust of the cave day after day, a plan had begun to take shape in his mind.

§

A week later, Sandro was walking home from the cinema. As he turned a corner onto the boulevard, the street appeared darker and more deserted than usual. It was abnormally quiet. On the corner stood an old woman holding a tray of wooden matches. As he tossed his coin on her tray and took a box of matches, she glanced up. Something had drawn her attention. Her eyes were frightened and Sandro, too, turned to look down the street.

A huge black horse, riderless, charged down the middle of the empty boulevard. Its eyes were fierce, its mouth foaming. Its hoofs thundered, the sound echoing off nearby buildings as sparks flew from the cobblestones. It roared past like a locomotive, then disappeared into the night.

Seconds later, a ragged crowd of workers rounded the corner, the air filling with panic. They were running toward him.

"What is it?" Sandro asked one of them. "*Qué pasa?*"

"After the meeting ... *la policía* ... they opened fire!" The thin man, his eyes terror-stricken, brought his hands to his head and pulled madly at his hair. "It was terrible, terrible. I saw two comrades fall in front of me. There was blood in the street. We did nothing, nothing at all, but they began shooting. Why?"

Sandro knew Jorge had gone to the meeting. He leaped into the crowd.

As he ran against a sea of faces, he stopped two students he knew from the school and blurted, "Jorge Sentis. Do you know him? Have you seen him?"

They shook their heads and hurried on.

Finally, two blocks from the hall, he saw Teresa. "Have you seen Jorge?"

Breathless, she leaned toward him, resting both hands on his shoulders, her head against his chest. Once she could speak, she turned and pointed down the street. "I saw him go down that alley. He was bent over, limping. Be careful, the *policía* are everywhere."

Sandro ran, then paused at the alley's mouth and glanced back. Teresa was following, but he plunged into the darkness without waiting for her. He could barely make out a form lying on the ground ahead of him. Jorge's eyes were wide, his head turned to the side. He lay on his stomach.

"Jorge, Jorge ..."

Sandro, breathing heavily, wanted to help, but was afraid to touch him.

"Sandro, *ay*! They shot me, in the leg. I was never lucky."

"Can you walk? You must get to a doctor. Come."

But Jorge simply rolled onto his back. Sandro watched with horror as blood pooled on the cobblestones. Jorge groaned and closed his eyes.

When he opened them again, Sandro hovering above him, he grabbed Sandro's shirt and said, with fierce conviction, "Go home, Sandro! Go home!" Then he fainted.

Jorge's pant leg was soaked with blood. Bending on one knee, Sandro lifted his friend and angled him over his shoulder. Jorge was small and weighed less than Sandro. "Follow me — my apartment is close by," Teresa said from behind.

The swell of people had grown more turbulent and they were swept up in it. Several streets away, they heard an exchange of gunfire. Sandro was sweating and felt dizzy.

Teresa put her hand on his arm. "It's not far. This way." A worker ran past, shouting, "They're coming! They're coming!"

Two men carrying revolvers hurried in the opposite direction and ducked into a doorway. A phalanx of Guardia Civil surged down the boulevard, several on horses. Half a block ahead of them, Sandro and Teresa turned down a side street and entered her building.

Moments later, Teresa closed her apartment door and leaned against it, trying to catch her breath. Sandro looked for a place to put Jorge. "On the bed," she pointed.

"He needs a doctor." He placed Jorge on the narrow bed. "I think he's lost a lot of blood."

"I know one who won't ask questions. I'll go for him."

"Now?"

"What choice do we have?"

§

The doctor leaned over Jorge who was moaning in agony. The doctor paused. "You are sure he is a comrade? Otherwise I won't touch him."

Teresa nodded. She leaned her head against the wall and slumped to the floor. "We have just begun and already it is over, finished. There will be a coup. The generals will take the side of the bourgeoisie, as always. They will crush the Revolution."

Sandro looked at her. "What makes you so sure?"

"You are an innocent, Sandro. Our numbers are greater, but we idealists have too many opinions; we are divided among ourselves." She stared at the floor and shook her head. "Our opinions won't mean anything if we cannot agree on a plan for the future. Those who cling to the past have the advantage of cohesion. Those in power know what they want because they have had it all along, while those who want Revolution each have our own dream of the future."

She turned her face to the window. Her deep, black eyes and heavy eyebrows drew him to her, but it was also her intelligence — he had recognized it the first time he saw her in the café.

The doctor turned to them, wiping his hands on a towel. He was young and wore thick glasses. "He'll be all right. Lost a fair bit of blood. I got the bullet out of his thigh, but he will need close supervision for a while."

Sandro thanked him, but the doctor waved him off.

A short while later, the threesome sat at a wooden table eating blood sausage and bread and drinking *vi negre*, wine true to its name, so dark it was almost black. Teresa gazed into her cup. When she looked up, she thought, *He looks like a fanatic, this doctor.*

At that moment, the doctor raised his cup and shouted, "To the *Revolución!*"

§

After the doctor left, they sat for a long time in silence. Jorge groaned in a half sleep. Sandro stood, went to the bed and put his hand on his friend's forehead, then walked back to his chair. "There are bloodstains on the bed."

Teresa shrugged. "You were both at the university?"

"No, at the trades school. Engineering. I came here from my village, Arcasella, in Asturias on the north coast. And you?"

"A small village called Sarasa, to the north of the city."

"I remember seeing you a few times in the café with Jorge, but I never caught your full name."

She gazed at him and smiled. "My name is Teresa Maza."

"I am Sandro Risco Cánovas."

"Sandro is an Italian name. *Por qué?*"

"My father is a fisherman. Many years ago he saved an Italian sailor who was shipwrecked near our village. They became friends. I am named for him."

"It's a lovely name."

"I am used to it." He paused. "You live here alone?"

"This was my great-aunt's apartment. I lived with her until she died two months ago. She was very old. Now my family wants me to return home, but it is impossible."

Sandro went to the window. The street was black. "What now?"

"Jorge can stay here. When he is feeling better, you can take him to his apartment. You must stay here tonight as well. The streets may appear quiet, but they are not safe. Not yet."

§

Exhausted, but too excited to sleep, they talked until dawn of politics, philosophy, home. She told him about her family, the village where she grew up. He told her about Arcasella, the sweep of curving beach, the nearby mountains, his rugged yet gentle father, his mother's garden. He told her of his brother Pedro, two years younger yet more than a brother.

Sandro took a sip of wine. "Jorge said you have been involved with the anarchists."

She glanced sideways at him. "For all I know you are a spy."

"Not likely. I consider myself apolitical." Sandro confessed.

"You don't want to dirty your hands with politics?"

He shook his head. "Not at all."

"I will not waste my breath trying to convince you. But please, tell no one that you know me. My work is important to me even if it isn't to you." She looked up at the window. "It will soon be morning. Perhaps you should go. Come back this evening — to see Jorge, I mean. I will keep a close watch on him until then."

"You will follow the doctor's instructions, change the dressing?"

"Of course."

After Sandro left, Teresa stood at the window, her arms folded over her chest, watching him walk up the street. *This should not have happened now. There is too much to accomplish. This ... this fool comes into my life ... I cannot afford to play the stunned schoolgirl.* "Damn," she said aloud, with more resignation than anger.

§

That evening Sandro returned to her apartment to check on Jorge and to join Teresa for a meal of cod stew. He told her why he had come to Barcelona. He told her about the summer he spent with Jorge in the cave in the mountains. He went on and on, swallowing her with his eyes.

Teresa listened closely and intently. "Tell me everything," she said. "I want to know everything about you."

§

The priest in Arcasella considered himself a modern man. In a village of poor fishermen, he was a man of great intelligence, a man who had been to university, a man who lived in a world utterly divorced from the sea. It was this Padre Esteban who had convinced a former villager, who had grown rich raising cattle in Argentina, that a scholarship fund would be the just way to share his good fortune. Once the fund was established, the priest had no trouble choosing Sandro, son of Agustín and Mercedes, to be the first student to benefit from the man's kindness. Sandro had stood out in the sleepy school where the priest taught everything from Latin and catechism to literature and arithmetic. Padre Esteban took Sandro aside after class one day and sat him down.

As Sandro listened attentively, Padre Esteban said, "You have been chosen for a great honour, Sandro, by a good man in our village. You never knew him — you were a baby when he lived here — but he knows your family. He is a most generous man. You should be proud. The people here, your parents and the others, know little of the outside world. Some of them believe that God means them to be poor, but I do not believe this. I believe they should always have enough to eat and a good education, a better one than they could attain from a simple priest. And better houses and electricity. You are an intelligent boy, Sandro. I had hoped you might have a calling to the priesthood, but I do not believe that is meant to be. You could help change things here, improve the lives of the villagers, become an engineer. Perhaps you will return and build a dam here for electricity. You will go to the technical school in two years, and then we shall see."

Sandro nodded and bowed his head. "I will try to repay your faith in me, Father."

In his first two years at the *Universidad Politécnica* in Barcelona, Sandro tackled his subjects with vigour. His mother, born in Barcelona, had always spoken Catalan at home so the language of the city was no barrier. It was his mother who had decided he would study there rather than in Madrid. She had a brother there, in the navy, who would keep an eye on him.

Sandro enjoyed the pulsating life of the city and made friends quickly, drinking coffee on the Ramblas with Jorge and others.

When he met Professor Gomez, a strapping man, slightly bent with age and years of poring over texts, he invited Sandro and Jorge to work for him in the cave at Linares. He said, "The pay is fair, but you will not grow rich."

When Sandro first arrived with Jorge in the town of Altamira in Cantabria, he was told its famous caves drew experts and visitors from around the world. The guests were wealthy by village standards, professors and rich tourists who needed lodging, food and entertainment. The influx of money meant better education for the local children, better employment, better futures. Without the caves, Altamira would have been just another dusty, backward village, not unlike his own Arcasella.

Professor Gomez told them how numerous caves with Paleolithic art had been discovered in the second half of the nineteenth century. The French paleontologist Harle and the historian Carthailac had pronounced the discoveries frauds at first, but by the turn of the century the pendulum had swung the other way. So many works were being discovered in caves in France and Spain that the experts reversed their opinions. Dozens of new sites were found, studied, restudied and declared genuine.

Sandro and Jorge traveled on to Linares and the cave that so interested Gomez. For three months, they helped to measure and copy the paintings that covered the cave walls and ceilings — horses, bison, bulls, aurochs, deer, bears, mastodons, geometric shapes, clusters of dots — all in a wide array of earthy colours, beautifully rendered, magnificently preserved. They collected twenty-two boxes of artifacts and materials from the cave floor. They found several Venus figures, dozens of flints, stone lamps. Gomez speculated that the cave inhabitants had filled the lamps with grease or some sort of oil, using a sprig of juniper or another plant for a wick. Anything organic of that sort, of course, had long ago turned to dust.

They found a variety of other materials from the period: small stone sculptures of various beasts; a single phallus; a few chunks of pigment, ochre and hematite; various scattered pieces of charcoal; many bones, mostly of reindeer, which appeared to be their main diet (although, strangely, no reindeer appeared among these paintings); a bit of fish bone; a few shells, which they believed might have been used to hold powdered pigment; other oddments. They labeled and categorized everything.

On Sandro's first afternoon at the site, it was scorching, the sky a blazing white. The leaves on the few nearby trees were grey with the heat and coated with dust from farmers passing by the cave entrance, pulling produce or stones or huge jugs of wine in donkey carts.

Professor Gomez said their work was extremely important, though tedious and demanding great patience. Sandro had removed the soil, bit by bit, from the earth floor beneath the paintings, sifting through it for objects of interest. Each time he came across a piece of bone or a bit of sculpture, he noted its precise location in a notebook, described it and gave it a number. He tied a tag with the same number around the object. The soil separated from the objects was discarded in barrels and removed at the end of each day.

Sandro and Jorge worked out a routine. They entered the cave early in the morning and walked for ten minutes until they came to a place where the cave split. Sandro took the left-hand corridor, while Jorge turned right. The professor had insisted they work in separate rooms for fear they would end up talking more than working. They rejoined each other in the late afternoon and had dinner in the evening at the home of a woman who boarded them in the village.

Every day, Sandro sat alone, deep in a small chamber under the earth, jotting down measurements, gazing through a magnifying glass, taking notes, sketching the images or sifting and shoveling soil into barrels. At night, just before sleep swallowed him, he closed his eyes and the animals he had seen on the cave walls gathered and swirled through the dark, like phosphorescence on the sea. Early the next morning he would be back inside the Earth's damp womb, staring at the wall, at the figures sliding in and out of each other.

The seed had been planted and he nurtured it, watched as it threw out a tiny white root and slowly began to split its shell. Here, deep in the earth, he refined his plan, worked out the details from beginning to end.

Lying in the cave on his back in the dirt, Sandro stared at a bull, oddly upside down, near the edge of the cave's sloping ceiling. In the flickering pulses of candlelight along the stone walls, he gazed at the pleasing warm black and brown pigments. It had been drawn with great skill and vision.

Will I be capable of replicating such beauty? Or will I be discovered, called a fool, an embarrassment to my family, my village?

The bull lacked hooves — its legs were cut off three-quarters of the way down. As a result the beast seemed to float, was not of the Earth at all.

What does it remind me of? Yes, of course — the chips of crystal and mica at the snout, the eye, the tips of horns, tail. This bull isn't deep inside the Earth at all. It's moving through the heavens ... the line of dots across the ceiling is the dust of the Milky Way.

As a child he had lain at night on a sloping hillside, gazing at the stars, but there deep in the Earth he also looked at Taurus, the Bull. He felt the steam from its nostrils, the thunder of its invisible hooves. It stared at him, its horns glinting, its tendons and muscles like twisted cloth or strands of seaweed holding its bones in place, its tail a length of rope but alive, a whip of hair-covered leather. It charged along the cave wall in flickering light and shadow. Absolutely still, it moved through time.

He laughed, but the noise died quickly in the hard bends of the stone galleries. He knew his plan was ridiculous. It would be so much work — replicating the drawings, maintaining the deception. He laughed because, though he saw himself as a lazy man, he knew it would be done.

§

The sun was tangled in the branches of an apple tree, the afternoon warm and without clouds. Sandro saw Professor Gomez and Jorge, at the foot of the hill, talking to several workmen.

The wind lifted a corner of the page Sandro was holding. With a pencil he drew another black line on a page already filled with a flurry of strokes, moving from left to right, a dip, a hump, a shallow descent. He barely looked at it before trying again. He wished to draw the line in a fluid motion, a single stroke. In one curve of the hand, one curl of the fingers, he drove himself to depict the humped back of a bull. He wanted the line, utterly clean and clear, to draw itself; the horns, the legs, head, tail came later. He worked intensely. He drew the single curved line again, his hand intuiting the stroke through repetition.

Hearing the tinkle of a bell, he slipped the sketchbook and pencil into a cloth sack. As a donkey passed on the path, Sandro "hallooed" to the farmer, who nodded his head and waved his hand. Sandro watched the sway of the animal, the motion of its legs, the roll of its haunches. When the farmer and his mount disappeared around a curve, he pulled out the sketchbook, brushed his black hair out of his eyes and set to work again.

The summer eventually came to an end. At night, the cool mountain air rose as mist from the narrow valleys. Jorge left for Barcelona and a week later Sandro prepared to leave for Arcasella before heading back to Barcelona himself.

§

Ignacio, Professor Gomez's simple-minded hired man, loaded the wooden boxes and barrels of dirt on the cart as if they were filled with nothing heavier than dried chaff. Sandro knew he would ask no questions.

"Eight barrels of soil today, Ignacio."

In an hour he had removed the eight barrels and Sandro pointed out the wooden crates that were to be taken to the professor's storage shed.

"Numbers 16, 17 and 18, plus those unnumbered ones."

Ignacio picked up one wooden box and placed it on top of another. "*Senor Profesor* has gone to Madrid today?"

"Yes. He left this morning. I will go with you to the shed to unload. We must hurry to make it to the post office before closing time."

The wooden wheels of the cart squeaked down the hill, the mule grunted, its ears flicked away flies. At the shed, Sandro showed Ignacio where to stack the boxes. When he began unloading the unnumbered crates, Sandro stopped him.

"Not those. Those we take to the post."

On earlier visits to the shed, Sandro had noticed several crates with containers of lamp oil and another of explosives. He had assembled a box with a dozen tins of oil, as well as twenty sticks of dynamite that might prove useful given the uncertain future.

Sandro's heart beat quickly as the postman filled out the address on the form. The man printed the letters with difficulty — ARCASELLA. He lifted his head from the page at the completion of each letter, swallowed, sighed, rested and then returned to the struggle. Sandro prayed that no one he knew from the village would come through the door. How would he explain the shipment of ten large wooden boxes? His personal effects? His books? Trinkets he had bought in the village? No, anything he could say would sound ridiculous. Luckily, the postmaster was a mute. He also had little more intelligence than a mule and like Ignacio, who was, in fact, his brother, he was not in the habit of prying into the lives of visitors.

"When will they go out?" Sandro asked.

The postmaster gave him a blank look, then turned to Ignacio, who interpreted his brother's eye movements and hand gestures to mean that the boxes would be moving along the next morning.

The postmaster shook his head vigorously and glared at Ignacio.

"Oh, excuse me, *Don* Sandro, Thursday morning."

Again, the postmaster shook his head and this time slammed his fist on the counter.

"Yes, no, it is tomorrow morning."

Sandro spoke. "Ignacio, tomorrow *is* Thursday."

Ignacio shrugged his shoulders, turned and walked out the door.

That evening Sandro left the village in the Pyrenees and traveled to Arcasella, arriving several days before the load of boxes he had shipped. When the boxes arrived, he used his father's cart to pick them up from the harbour and haul them to the small family barn. Late that night, with Pedro's help, he took them by cart to the edge of the forest and they hauled them into the cave. When they were finished, Sandro made sure that the cave entrance was completely hidden.

"I have a plan," he told Pedro, but said no more.

§

For the next week, Sandro spent every evening with Teresa, helping to care for Jorge and talking long into the night. They had supper together, Teresa cooking up *cocido* (a stew of pork, chickpeas, bacon and potatoes), or salted cod in tomatoes, or *arros negre* (black rice cooked in squid's ink). Once, he went into the kitchen to look into a pot and she brandished a knife at him. "Get out," she said, "all men are idiots in the kitchen."

He listened to her slightly husky voice, like unpolished silver, and thought, *I have never actually heard a voice until now.* It was as if her presence had woken him from a deep sleep. They did nothing special — talked, ate, changed Jorge's dressing — and yet, it was enough.

He took nothing for granted, but each evening she asked him to stay through the night as the hour had grown late and she was afraid the Guardias would stop him and ask difficult questions. Finally, at the end of a week, he headed home to spend a night in his own bed.

§

The next morning, Sandro lay for a long time in bed looking at the sunlight on the wall of his room and the dust motes in the air. The sound of voices in the street floated up to him. His sensations were precise and clear. He loved every detail of the world because he had fallen in love with one small part of it.

The moment he had set eyes on her, he knew fate had ordained their future together. He also knew that if he admitted any of this to Teresa, she would accuse him of yielding to romantic notions.

Despite his conviction and desire, he would have to wait.

He dressed slowly, in a state of delicious tension.

When he headed out into the sunlit street, in the direction of the post office, he came upon a crowd.

"What is it?" he asked one of the men.

"A list of people sought by the authorities." The man pointed to a bulletin posted on the door, removed his cap and wiped his brow. "Any fool that answers this summons will be in jail by tomorrow." The labourer addressed the crowd with authority: "Ignore it. Do not go. If your name is on the list, go into hiding, or leave the city. If no one reports, what can they do? But do not linger. I know two people on the list who have already been arrested, early this morning."

Sandro worked his way to the front of the crowd. He scanned the names, expecting to come across Jorge's, or possibly even Teresa's, but he stopped short: Jorge's name was indeed on the list, but his own name was on it as well. Guilty for being a friend of Jorge's.

At home, he gathered a few effects in a small suitcase, including his pigments, sketchbook and the money he kept under the loose lining of his trunk. He went to the window and looked down. A pair of Guardia Civil on horses were working their way up the street, stopping people, questioning them. *I must get to Teresa's.* He recalled her skin, her jet-black hair, her voice, her subtle scent. *"In jail by morning, do not linger."* Sandro scanned the street again; the Guardia Civil had turned down a side street.

As he hurried down the steps, he noticed Jorge's red bicycle at the bottom of the stairwell and immediately changed his plans. *Jorge warned me, told me to go home.* He tied his suitcase to its carrier with a worn rope. *Teresa, please forgive me.*

The Saint James Way

Sandro, on Jorge's bicycle, rolls down a long, sweetly curving road in spring sunlight, a twist here, another longer twist there, a stream gurgling alongside.

This old bicycle will miss the excitement of delivering manifestos, posters, love letters, maybe even a few homemade bombas.

Sandro's legs pump the pedals, the bicycle's rubber-ringed orbits sing.

Through the city streets and into the outskirts Sandro laboured like a demon, exhibiting all the frenzied strength of youth without raising a pearl of sweat.

In that first long climb the muscles of his thighs hardened and tightened as he strained with all his might, imagining himself a yellow shirt in Le Tour de France. As he crested the hill, the town of Lerida and the countryside unfolded before him: a copse of oak trees and fields running down to a wide valley where a river shimmered with sunlight.

They sail now, bicycle and man fused into a single beast, a single hinged bi-form machine. He stops pedaling and simply glides, a split-tailed swallow, a *golondrina* sluicing down the wind in wide, sweet arcs, soft spirals and willowy curves.

At the bottom, by the side of a stream, he stops and sets the bike gently against a tree before taking a pear from his bag. He cups the water curling over stones and slakes his thirst.

Sandro looks at the bicycle. *What to call it? Babieca? Bucephalus? Rocinante? No ... Libertad? Yes. Libertad. Freedom.*

§

Sandro lay in thick grass under the stars, a scratchy green blanket pulled up to his chin, his head resting on his suitcase. His face and skull looked sculpted, as if he was a stone figure sleeping on a saint's sarcophagus. He could pass for a Castilian, with his black wavy hair, straight nose and mournful eyes.

Will Teresa understand why I had to run? What must she think of me? Perhaps she saw my name on the list and knows I had to escape. Tomorrow morning I will write to her and explain everything.

He surveyed the sky.

I'll follow the Saint James Way, pretend I'm on the pilgrimage to Santiago de Compostela, but I'll turn north at León and head for the coast.

§

As she had dozens of times that morning, Teresa walked to the window and looked down at the street. *Why did he not come last night? Where is he? If he doesn't show, I'll go ...*

A solid double-knock sounded on Teresa's door. She walked to the door, opened it tentatively. Standing in the hall were two Guardia Civil, tall policemen with hard eyes, leather boots and starched uniforms.

"*Señorita*," one of them said, bowing slightly. "We are seeking two men who were seen in this area last week. One Jorge Sentis, and his accomplice, Sandro Cánovas. Have you seen them?"

"No. I do not know these men."

A moan came from the bedroom, where Jorge had awoken in pain.

"Who is that?" Both Guardias glanced into the apartment, trying to see through the half-light.

"My sister, she has the fever. I am watching over her."

"I see. Excuse us, then, for disturbing you."

Both men bowed graciously and left. Teresa closed the door slowly, trying to remain calm.

Twenty minutes later, she stole out into the street and walked briskly to Sandro's boarding-house. She held her blouse tight at her neck. The landlady, a full-faced matron with deep-set eyes, met her at the door.

"Can you tell me, *por favor*, where I might find Sandro Cánovas?"

"Oh, he's a popular fellow today. First the *policía* and now a young lady. As I told the Guardias, he left yesterday morning. On a bicycle. Didn't say where he was headed, but had a suitcase with him. He never tells me where he's going and I don't ask. If you see him, remind him his rent is due tomorrow."

§

A pilgrim in a full-length black cape, his hair long, a broad-brimmed black hat on his head to protect against the fist of the sun, trudged up the hill ahead of Sandro. In his hand he gripped a fresh green staff, a gourd tied to it for dipping water. A satchel hung over his left shoulder. "Look at this fellow," Sandro whispered under his breath. "Like a bit of Old Testament."

"*Hola!*" Sandro shouted as he approached.

The man turned and nodded a greeting. He halted for a moment as Sandro dismounted and then the two continued their climb on foot, Sandro pushing the bicycle as they spoke. A scallop shell was fastened to the front of the pilgrim's cape.

"Heading to Santiago de Compostela?"

"It would not be a lie." The *peregrino* smiled through his moustache and beard, wide gaps between his teeth, his red face more that of a debauchee than a saint.

"Where do you come from?"

"Near Castellón. I work there as a farmer's hand. And you?"

"I left Barcelona a short time ago. I'm on my way back to my village. But for now I, too, am a pilgrim."

"I see. We both have a long journey ahead of us, then. I hope we don't encounter any fighting. It might delay us. I need the *compostellana* for its plenary indulgence."

"*Compostellana?*"

"The document that confirms I have completed the pilgrimage."

"Are you a great sinner?"

"You don't know the half of it."

He did not seem to want to elaborate, so Sandro did not pry.

"You mentioned fighting. What have you heard?"

"Yesterday evening, at an inn, some locals said that the army is about to revolt. There have been assassinations. People taken from their beds and never seen again. The cemeteries are sprouting fresh graves overnight."

"This is bad news."

"If the fighting spreads, I might have to return home, my sins unpurged."

"Things have started up more quickly than I expected."

"I saw two detachments of Guardia Civil yesterday morning. Did you see them too?"

"No. They may have turned off the road."

"What is your name?"

Sandro paused. "My name? *Me llamo...* Julio."

They shook hands, an odd formality it seemed to Sandro in this abandoned countryside. The pilgrim, who was plump and thick-lipped, said, "They call me Salvador."

They walked a while, hearing only the occasional peep of a thrush and the squeak of the bicycle's wheels.

Salvador sighed. "The anti-clericals have burned churches, broken windows, slashed paintings, drunk the holy wine. It is an abomination."

"Yes, atrocious."

"You are against the Republic, then?"

"No, I could not say that."

"Are you a communist?"

"No, not that, either."

"An anarchist?"

"No, definitely not."

"Then what are you?"

"A bicyclist." Sandro's face broke into a wide smile.

The pilgrim burst out laughing and asked Sandro to share his lunch.

They sat on the side of the road and Salvador opened his satchel. "I have only some bread and ham and two apples."

"I can contribute hazelnuts and a square of cheese." Sandro rummaged in the bag, "as well as a flask of wine, rough and red as bull's blood, but nourishing nonetheless."

"*Maravilloso.*"

They ate and talked, the pines above them sighing in the breeze, a few wisps of cloud sweeping across the sky.

Salvador leaned on one elbow as he ate. "Last night I dreamed of minced meat, lentils, eggs and bacon, as well as pigeon. Food has been my greatest sacrifice — I am hungry all the time."

"Mmm." Sandro cut a slice of white cheese with his knife and offered it. "I miss the foamy beer my friend and I used to buy from the street vendors in Barcelona. That and a girl. I sleep each night like a stone deep underwater, so I have no energy for lovemaking in any case. My legs have finally stopped twitching at night from the strain of my daily exertions."

Salvador frowned. "Do not speak of women in my presence."

"Why?"

"It reminds me of my unspeakable sins."

"Your secrets are your own."

Salvador looked up and gazed at the distant horizon. "The good padre in our village sent me on this journey because ... because ... I ... I .... No. They are unspeakable."

Sandro paused, the knife blade in the cheese. "In any case, you are now on the road to redemption, yes? The padre has shown you the way to mercy."

Salvador gritted his teeth. "I must not."

When Sandro said, "Perhaps you really should speak about them," Salvador shook his head.

"Unspeakable," he mumbled and flopped back onto the ground.

Sandro rose, bid Salvador farewell, hopped onto Libertad and continued his journey west.

§

At dusk, the sun beyond the hills, the landscape looked like hammered copper. It had been a day of easy riding: a flat stretch, empty country, Libertad's chain newly oiled.

A long way off, Sandro saw two men in a copse of oak trees.

As he approached, a Guardia Civil waved him over. "Have you any bullets?" he shouted when Sandro was still some distance away. Sandro shook his head. He saw that the other man, older than the Guardia, wiry and mean-looking with a cut under his eye, was a prisoner. He was tied to a chestnut tree with a sturdy rope. "No bullets?" the Guardia repeated as Sandro dismounted and held his bike.

"No. *Por qué?*"

"I am to execute this prisoner and the fools have left me here with no bullets. Am I to beat him to death with my rifle?" The Guardia's boots were torn and ragged, his uniform spotted, a cap pushed back on a head of wiry, brown hair. "*Mierda!* What am I to do?"

"Has there been fighting?"

"Not yet. No one has actually declared war, yet everyone knows it is coming. Two nights ago this one slit the throats of two of my best friends. And now ... Perhaps I will have to throttle him with my bare hands."

The prisoner, who looked like a hunted dog, spit at him and growled. "Try it."

The Guardia turned his back on his charge. "Which side will you be joining?"

Sandro shuffled his feet. "I don't know. First I must get home to my village."

"Smart fellow. Listen. Stay out of it. On one side are asses like me, on the other, pigs like him." He nodded his head toward the prisoner. "My captain said that if I don't return with the ears of this prisoner, he'll know that I am a coward and will shoot me."

"What will you do with him?"

"I will have to leave him here."

"Tied to the tree? There is no one around. No one will hear him calling."

"But if I untie him, he'll grab me by the throat. *Mierda!*"

Sandro scratched his head. He motioned the young Guardia to lean close and whispered in his ear.

A few minutes later the Guardia walked off, heading for the distant hills. He turned and waved. Sandro leaned Libertad against a tree, loosened the knots and turned to hop on the bike. The prisoner ripped at his bonds and was free in moments. Sandro raced to Libertad and jumped on. The bike shot across the field and onto the road, the prisoner cursing behind him.

§

Sandro lay back in the grass on the west side of a hill under the night sky, the stars like candles beating against the dark in a vast cathedral. They reminded Sandro of the cave at Linares.

One day he had gone in search of Jorge, but just as he approached his chamber he realized he would have to get down on his hands and knees to crawl through a narrow opening. After about four metres, the low passage took a hard turn to the right and Sandro entered a high vault. He scanned the long stone hall lit by dozens of candles stuck to boulders among the stalagmites. The pulse and flicker of light illuminated a herd of wild horses tumbling along the right wall and a pair of woolly mammoths gamboling on the left.

But where was Jorge? It felt like a sacrilege to raise his voice against the deep silence. "Jorge," he whispered. He moved carefully through the forest of lights. "Jorge."

He switched the lamp to his left hand and was startled to see Jorge's inert shape lying in the distance against the back wall. Dios mío, *is he dead? He must have fallen asleep.* He edged closer, the light tossing his shadow in among the animals along the walls. "Jorge?" The candles pulsed, the beasts flickered, turned their heads and leaped through light.

Teresa,

Please forgive me. I was unable to come to you as planned. I was forced to flee the city. I was on the police list and feared I would be arrested if I answered the summons. I had no choice. I'm sorry to leave you alone with Jorge. I am sure you have your own worries.

It is terribly lonely on these dusty roads, under the black, burning sun. I am now a single thread of muscle, seven shades browner, and many kilograms lighter. I wonder if you will recognize me when next we meet.

I have been sleeping out-of-doors under the blanket of stars, the Milky Way stretching across the sky. I cannot tell you where I am headed, in case the policía should find this, and you are unable to write to me, but I will find a way to let you know of my progress.

Until then,
Sandro

§

The sprocket of the sun glitters and spins in the morning heavens, one tooth after another making the world roll round, Libertad's wheels in harmony, oiled, noiseless.

The road spirals into brilliant skies.

We move like mad angels through a crazed and ambiguous landscape, insanely blessed.

§

As the sun's heat grew bothersome, Sandro pedaled into the ancient town of Puente la Reina, its stone buildings like a herd of old goats gathered by the Arga river. The quiet town nestled among soft violet hills about forty kilometres west and south of Pamplona, a city he skirted, fearing the residents might have heard something of him, Sandro Risco Cánovas, the fugitive from Barcelona.

He glided down into the sleepy streets of the town — an overgrown village, really — and came to a stop at an inn. There he ate and booked lodging for the night.

The innkeeper told him that the town was a crossroads where the two pilgrim routes, the Camino Aragonés and the Camino Navarro, join.

Near the medieval bridge at the western edge of the town, Sandro discovered a simple, slightly decrepit Romanesque church that had been converted into a cinema. A poster on the wooden door of the church announced the Marx Brothers in *Sopa de Ganso*.

§

Later, after the film, as he wheeled Libertad through the medieval gateway and onto the six-span bridge, Sandro encountered a dark wide-eyed boy, about nine years old.

"*Señor*, it is a very fine *bicicleta*."

"Yes. I trust it will get me all the way home."

"Where is that?"

"Far away, by the sea. And you?"

"We have no home. We are *gitanos*. Tomorrow we leave for France. We will cross the border. My mama says the air here smells of blood."

Sandro bit his lower lip and looked closely at the boy's smooth face. His shock of black hair looked as if it had never seen a comb. Sandro nodded a "hello" as a shopkeeper and his wife passed arm in arm.

When they had gone the boy spoke again. "Yesterday I saw a dead man in the field near the roadblock."

"What roadblock?"

The boy pointed over the bridge. "That way, about a half-hour cart ride. Guardia Civil are stopping everyone and taking many of the men away. We were lucky. I was too young and my papa has a wooden leg. Sometimes they come into town searching for troublemakers to send off to the army."

"Are you sure about this?"

"Yes. We have been camping nearby in the forest for a week. Come ask my papa, he will tell you."

"Listen, what's your name?"

"Chaleco."

"Come with me to the inn and I will fetch my bag and then you can show me the way to your camp."

§

As they passed over the bridge and out of the town, Sandro followed Chaleco down a path until they arrived at a small clearing littered with half a dozen covered carts, a makeshift pen for goats and a few horses tied to trees. Two men sat on logs around a fire that spat sparks at the stars. A dozen children gathered and ran up to Chaleco and Sandro.

"Who is he?"

"You will see," Chaleco said over his shoulder as they moved toward the men.

"Papa, this is Sandro. He is trying to get home to his village by the sea. Will the Guardias at the roadblock arrest him?"

A grizzled-looking man with a heavily-lined face nodded to Sandro and smiled. "*Hola*. Please sit. I am Carlos Mantilla Lopez. Where is your home?"

"Arcasella, near Oviedo."

"Yes, I know this place. It will be very difficult. Soon the fighting will begin. I am sure of it. You will have some *vino*, yes?" He passed Sandro a bulging wineskin. The silent old man next to Carlos drank as well.

"If you knew the paths as we *gitanos* know them you could reach your home without difficulty, as easily as a ghost passing through water. Unfortunately for you we are not headed your way. We leave soon for *Francia*. We know the mountain trails. No one knows we are here, no one will ever know that we have left. We fly across borders like birds."

"But if the Guardias stop me, I will tell them I am on a holy pilgrimage to Santiago."

"No. Better to try to avoid them if you can. You could tell them that your bicycle is the angel Gabriel and they would just nod, take you behind a tree and put a bullet in your head. They would say you are a simple madman and therefore of use to no one."

"Then what am I to do?"

"Tomorrow, with the first light, I will take you to a place where you can see the roadblock from a distance and you can judge for yourself. To see is to believe, as Saint Thomas says. Then I will show you a trail that will help you avoid other Guardias. You should travel at night."

He turned and adjusted his wooden leg, which, being too close to the fire, had started to smoke. He handed the old man the wineskin, leaned forward and stirred a pot. "Hungry?"

"I could eat."

Carlos took a crock from a pile resting on a nearby stone, filled it and handed it to Sandro.

"Ragout of snails."

The toothless old man turned and looked blearily at Sandro. "Stranger, you do not look like a *gitano*. What are you doing here?"

"Papa." Carlos glared at the old man. "He is not a savage. He is our guest. He wants to go home to his people, so do not insult him." He turned to Sandro. "You must forgive him, he is very old."

§

The next morning Sandro climbed down from the wagon where he had slept. A pair of hens danced a flamenco in the dust, scratching the ground and spreading their tail feathers. Carlos was ready and mounted his horse, pulling Chaleco up behind him.

Sandro followed them on Libertad, trying hard to keep up over the rough terrain. After an hour's ride they came to a hilltop field, a pile of boulders at one end. Carlos dismounted and limped ahead to peer between two rocks.

"There." He pointed.

Far below, the road snaked through a clutch of hills. The roadblock was immediately before a sharp rise. Two Guardia Civil rested heavily on black, thick-necked horses. Their hats looked like rectangular boxes and their leather boots came up almost to their knees. A cluster of other Guardias stood nearby.

Sandro, Carlos and Chaleco sat and watched for an hour. Finally a car approached. The Guardias turned and readied themselves. The first two Guardia Civil dismounted, approached the car and spoke to the driver. One of the guards opened the door and hauled out a cowering man, dragged him by the collar across the road and pushed him up against a tree. The guard took three paces back, pulled his *pistola* from his leather holster, raised his arm and fired. The man slumped forward. Four Guardias, taking one limb each, carried him to a nearby pit and swung him in.

"You must show me that secret path," Sandro whispered.

"*Sí,*" Carlos replied glumly.

When they returned to the encampment, Carlos drew an elaborate map for Sandro, sketching from memory the places where he remembered roadblocks or towns garrisoned with soldiers.

"Take side roads and paths that run parallel to the main route between here and León. Do not get caught with this *mapa*. The Guardias will shoot you on the spot. You must memorize it and then destroy it."

Sandro prepared to leave. "God be with you," said Carlos.

Chaleco handed Sandro a bag of food. "Perhaps we will meet in France one day and go to the cinema together."

Sandro smiled and nodded.

"*Adiós!*" Carlos shouted as Sandro pedaled down the forest path.

§

That day Sandro saw only three farmers, their donkeys and a single herd of sheep raising dust in the distance. The previous day he narrowly avoided a truck brimming with Guardias on the main road. Later that afternoon an airplane flew low to the ground and followed him for a while.

Another path crossed his a short distance ahead. A man on a donkey ambled by reading a book, completely oblivious to Sandro until he drew near. Suddenly, he slammed the book shut. "*Hola! Hola!*" the peasant shouted and waved, digging his heels into the side of his beast. "*Buenos días, amigo.*" He smiled toothily.

Sandro nodded greetings. "*Hola.* Where are you headed, *Señor?*"

"Here and there, so it is, so it is." The man looked as if he had been sleeping out-of-doors for months, his face as dry and weathered as a page from a well-thumbed manuscript.

The stranger had a beard that stretched from shoulder to shoulder and hung to his navel. As he moved or spoke, bits of bark, pine cones, pieces of torn paper, tobacco, hay and dust sifted from its grey bush.

"I am Domingo. As for you, I can tell you are not from here and have traveled long and hard already. By the look in your eye, I can see you fear you have a long way yet to go before reaching your destination. A *peregrino*, no doubt. In these hard times. Imagine."

"I am Sandro. I am traveling to Santiago ... making the pilgrimage."

"Ah, the slight hesitation, my friend, reveals your small lie. I can read you like a book. Not going to Santiago, no, no. Somewhere else. Not a spy, though; no more spy than me or Honey." He patted his donkey on the rump. "Not by the look of you. No, you can speak truth, for I am neither Carlist nor Falange nor *comunista*. Not even an anarchist, though I believe somewhere deep in my heart I would wave a tiny black flag, if any. Would you like something to read?"

"*Qué?* What do you mean?"

"Go ahead, change the subject, it matters not where you're headed, best to be safe in these dangerous times, and so on, and so on. Yes, something to read. In my bags here." He caressed a set of bloated saddlebags that hung over the rump of his donkey. Sliding off the beast with some difficulty, owing to his corpulence, he pulled the bags down and opened them, dumping the contents onto the ground. Books. Dozens of them. On politics, philosophy, religion. And political pamphlets: from the CNT, UGT, CEDA, the monarchists, socialists, syndicalists, Basque nationalists, one on how to make and stuff pork sausage. Some of the books were in rough shape, missing covers, dirty, dusty, torn, water-marked.

"Here. That's for you." Domingo handed Sandro a copy of Dante's *Inferno*, its front cover torn off. "Take it."

Sandro reached for it hesitantly. "*Gracias.*"

Domingo picked up a thick volume. "Marx. I've read him. Engels, too. Hegel. Once had a mongrel named Hegel. Read all of them. All the political theories. Machiavelli. Unamuno, Ruiz, Ortega y Gasset. Hobbes. The Greek classics. All the philosophers. No novels, though. Not for me. Got to think, got to think." Ripping a page from the volume of Marx he held in his hand, he leaned closer to Sandro as if to confide something. "Listen." He crumpled the page into a ball, popped it into his mouth, chewed it up and swallowed it. He then proceeded to give a ten-minute dissertation on Marx — a comparison of gold, silver and copper coins — that sounded lucid and intelligent enough to Sandro, although everything he knew about Marx, which wasn't much, he learned from Jorge in Barcelona as he leaned over the handlebars of his *bicicleta*.

Sandro stood with his mouth open. "I ... I don't know what to say."

"Nothing to be said. I'll tell you this, though, young friend. I've read all their theories and I have come to my own conclusion. Each and every one of them is as cracked as a man's ass. Wrong, wrong. There is but one political philosophy that will bear the test of time. I believe only in the *Estado Autónomo de la Lista de Correos*." He stood with his finger pointing to the sky.

"The Independent State of General Delivery?"

"*Sí, sí.*"

"Where is this place?"

Domingo walked to his donkey and touched her nose, "From here ...," then he took two strides to her tail, which he held up, "... to here."

Sandro tilted his head. "I see."

"Yes. A pure state of mobility, two metres square, that moves as I move. I keep it with me, *siempre*. I am a free man. I go where I wish. I pay no land tax. I have no army, no navy, no air force, no customs agents and no minister of agriculture. I am king and Honey, my donkey, is my royal vizier."

"A monarchy, then?"

"A *monarquía, sí*, of the enlightened sort. Nothing better for a man, nothing better. Marx be damned, Adam Smith, too. I should know, I am a defrocked priest, self-proclaimed, from the fair city of Salamanca, having taught philosophy and politics from the day the university opened its doors."

"That would be, roughly, seven hundred years ago."

"Aaach. Mathematics was never my forte. My count may be off somewhat. At any rate, I left of my own accord. I was too radical even for the radicals. Well, must be off. Books, books, books, so much to read," he mumbled as he stuffed volumes and pamphlets into the bags he threw over the donkey. As he rode off, he said over his shoulder, "Don't get caught up in all this, not for anything. Politics, pah! Bad stuff. Come on, Honey, move along now, that's a girl. Christ, what did I do with that volume by Lenin! Left it in Pamplona, or did I give it to that idiot friar? Damn, I'll be forced to return and steal it back ... Books, books, so much to read, so much ...," and he disappeared into the distance, still mumbling, as a sheet of paper slipped from his bag and drifted to the ground.

That evening Sandro found shelter under an overhang of rock to avoid the rain. He feared the damp would worsen Libertad's rusty spokes. Sandro waited out the storm in the dry, shallow cave, content to read Dante and enjoy a rare day of rest.

§

In Barcelona, rain beat on the windows of Teresa's apartment in the middle of the night. She awoke with a start, her heart pounding. She rose from her makeshift bed on the floor to go to Jorge. His face was soaked with sweat, his teeth clenched. Her hand on his forehead burned with his fever. *Is it gangrene setting in?* She pulled back the covers, reached for a bowl and cloth beside the bed and placed the cool compress on his forehead. *What was it he said to me today? You are Saint Teresa of Barcelona. Locked up for weeks in this place and yet he never complains.* She wrung out the cloth, wiped his chest, neck and upper back.

Why am I here, caring for Jorge when it is Sandro I dream of? I long to flee this city and now it is impossible. The roads are watched. Everything has gone wrong. She pulled the covers farther back and wiped around Jorge's wound. *Don't die now, not after all this. Sandro would never forgive me if I lost you. Where is he now, out there in the darkness?* A vehicle splashed along the unlit street.

The next morning Jorge's fever had broken. He sat up in bed, sipped milk from a metal cup. He stared at her. "I know you want to return to your village. You must leave me here — I will manage."

"I do want to go — this city is a hellhole — but I can't leave you, or my work. It wouldn't be right." She moved to the bed. "Look, I got you some books and tonight, after dark, I will take you out for some fresh air. Besides, tomorrow I am to begin work as a waitress at the Café Zona."

"The Zona? That is a soldiers' café."

"Yes, but the bartender, you see, sympathizes with us."

"It is important work you will be doing at the Zona, yes? The work of a spy?"

§

Sandro pedaled out of Navarre and into the Rioja region, west of Viana, and farther still into the spacious valley of the Ebro, around the city of Logroño and then back onto the pilgrims' way. He followed in the footsteps of Saint James the Moor-Slayer, *Sant Iago Matamoros*, whose ghost haunted these lands like a swirl of dust, the saint/soldier and his horse ever present on the plains, in the forests, on mountaintops, his long narrow face peeking out of doorways in every village. It was a road, had always been a road, littered with miracles and soaked with blood.

Sandro cycled through Navarrete and Najera, past their medieval monasteries and churches, onto a flat tableland of good soil rippling with fields of wheat, laced with orchards and vineyards. Skies blue in the morning, white by afternoon. Sandro and Libertad rode on and on. His strong legs pumped like pistons, Libertad's gears and wheels spun, kissing the road.

A few kilometres shy of Santo Domingo de la Calzada, the rope holding Sandro's suitcase broke and, before he could stop, its contents spilled across the road. He set the bicycle down, rushed back to the suitcase and stuffed his few belongings inside, taking care to check that his precious pigments were safe.

Sandro rode with the suitcase in one hand and steered with the other until he reached the outskirts of town. He saw a man sitting in front of a house, half asleep in the shade.

"*Hola*. Friend, do you know where I can purchase a length of rope?"

"Rope? Yes. There is a rope-maker." The man stood and shaded his eyes with his right hand, pointing the way for Sandro with his left. After asking directions several more times, Sandro found the house in question, near the road. The rope-maker was working in the dusty yard.

"*Buenas tardes*. I would like to buy a length of rope. Is it possible?"

"Not only is it possible, it is already done," replied the rope-maker, a balding stub of a man with short, fat fingers. At the far end of the bare yard sat an old woman, a scarecrow turning a wooden wheel. With ungainly bundles of flax wound around his middle, the rope-maker walked to the wheel and attached a long thread of flax to a spindle, pacing backward as he played out the flax into a string.

"You can have this rope when I have finished."

Sandro nodded and flopped down to wait, leaning the bike up against a fence. As the sun grew hot, Sandro shifted to a patch of shade by the house and fell asleep. When he awoke, he saw the rope-maker still walked back and forth, attaching threads to the spindle, taking one hundred paces backward (out of extreme boredom, Sandro counted them), tying the string to a pole, then doing the same again.

"How many strings must you gather?"

"*Doscientos*."

"Two hundred! When will you finish?"

"By dark. And then you will stay to supper."

Sandro agreed, resigned.

"You seem like a trustworthy fellow, so I will speak."

José discussed the merits of UGT, he argued the position of the Anarchist Doctrinal Vanguard, then the revolutionary communists of POUM, followed by the fascist JONS and the Catholic Party. "The workers have a point, I do not doubt it. I'm a worker myself; but the priest tells us to support CEDA, while the mayor here is *anarquista* and the flax pickers are *comunista*, but they dislike the Russians and the Italians even more, especially that horse's ass, Mussolini. I don't like him myself, as you can likely tell. But I am a simple man, who would care what I think?"

Sandro's neck grew tired from turning to watch the rope-maker pace back and forth. José halted. "*Maldita sea*! I've lost count. I will have to start over." He returned to the wheel. "Sometimes I think I should support PSUC," he began playing out the thread again, "because María Fraga Peiro is the head for this region and she is undoubtedly the most beautiful woman in the entire province, God and my mother (he nodded toward the old woman) forgive me for saying so. And you, who do you support?"

"*Sant Iago Matamoros.*"

José burst into such a fit of laughter he could not continue for several minutes. "*Ay.* You have made me lose my count again."

Sandro hung his head. Seeing this, José said, "There is a well at the back. You must be thirsty, my friend. And place your bicycle in the shed; this town is foul with thieves."

The well behind the house was next to a shady chestnut tree. He dipped a wooden bucket, drank, then opened the door of the tumbledown shed to find a place to lean the bicycle. Near the doorway, three kittens toyed with the end of a roll of rope. Sandro stopped. They had already unplaited half the roll.

§

After supper, José insisted on showing Sandro the tomb of Saint Dominic in the town's cathedral. "If you are on the great pilgrimage, you must see it. To miss it would be criminal."

Sandro fetched Libertad from the shed, invited José to sit on the crossbar and followed his directions into the main square. At the cathedral, José advised, "Bring the *bicicleta* in with you, there are thieves everywhere."

In the half-light they made their way to the tomb. Sandro was not in the habit of visiting the pilgrimage sites, but in this case he did not wish to arouse suspicion.

A heavy-set man with a thick moustache and dull eyes approached them.

"Ah, Police Inspector, good evening," José said in greeting.

"José." He nodded. "What are you doing in the cathedral tonight?"

"I have come to show this *peregrino*, my friend Sandro, our famous tomb."

"Indeed." He looked Sandro up and down. "And what are you doing in Santo Domingo de la Calzada?"

"He is on the pilgrimage to Santiago."

"José, please, I have asked the young man and I would like *him* to answer."

"Yes, I am on the pilgrimage."

"In such times as these? Imagine. It is hard to believe."

Sandro shrugged.

"How do we know you are not a spy? You have a foreign name. Italian, is it not?"

Sandro looked up at the sound of a clucking hen. "What is that?" Through the gloom of the cathedral he stared at a hen and rooster in a small cage high in the stone wall.

"They are the hen and rooster of Saint Dominic, or rather, descendants of the same."

The police inspector waved his hand. "Never mind that. How do we know you have not come here to draw up plans for an invasion?"

"Invasion by whom, Inspector?" José was oddly sincere.

"The point is," the inspector jabbed the index finger of his right hand into the open palm of his left, "is he a spy or a pilgrim?"

"Are those my only two choices?" Sandro asked.

"I know," José grinned, "let the hen and cock decide. You know the story, Inspector."

"Of course."

José explained to Sandro. "The miracle of Saint Dominic. The crowing of a roasted hen and cock attested to the innocence of a wrongly executed pilgrim."

"A little late, was it not? For all of them, I mean. The pilgrim already executed, the cock and hen already roasted."

José sighed. "Still, it was a miracle."

The police inspector took Sandro by the arm and led him toward the cage. Sandro pushed Libertad beside him.

The inspector paused. "I don't know. A bicycle in the church. That might be against the law."

"And a cock and hen is legal?" Sandro protested.

As they approached the cage, the cock leaned his head back and let out such a string of *crucka-rucka-roos* that candle flames throughout the cathedral wavered in response.

"*Un milagro!*" José gasped. "Another miracle!"

Suddenly several gunshots sounded from the nearby square. The police inspector ran off and Sandro and José hurried to a side exit. They sped back to José's house, secured the suitcase with the new rope, said their farewells and Sandro fled into the night.

§

Sandro felt the loneliness more keenly under the stars. Night riding was dangerous — a single rut or rock could bring his downfall — but the close call in the cathedral had made it a necessity. Because it was cooler at night, Sandro had more energy and made good time, encountering long stretches of straight road under a gibbous moon as he cycled into the region of Old Castile.

I am not about to stand passively before a firing squad for a crime I did not commit.

The fields stretched into the moonlight on each side of the road, a poplar in the distance striking a towering silhouette, and the stars sparkled like lanterns hung in the windows of a great inn.

In the heart of the night, when Sandro and Libertad sailed easily across the moon-swept landscape, there were times it felt as though the bicycle was finding its own way. Libertad was taking him home. Sandro had long conversations with Libertad — about Teresa, about Jorge, about his hopes and fears, speaking to it as one would speak to an intimate friend. And, in a sense, they *had* become friends, had shared both difficulty and danger on the road. And, like all good friends, Libertad listened well — and did not pass judgment as to Sandro's foolishness or good sense.

At dawn Sandro halted at the bottom of a long hill where a flicker of stream twisted through bushy hazels, slipped around rocks, tumbled over small rapids. He hid Libertad in the bushes, washed himself and changed into less dusty clothes. He scrubbed his pants and shirt in the stream and lay them out to dry on an inconspicuous rock. He ate a chunk of white cheese, some bread, drank from his wineskin and fell asleep.

§

Although Sandro traveled at night whenever he could, under the white fountain of the moon, occasionally, in overcast weather, he was forced to travel in daylight. On these days, he sensed a calculable danger in the air; there were more roadblocks to be skirted and farmers and peasants along the way appeared wary.

As he rounded a long curve, he pulled out the map, glanced at it one last time to confirm that he had memorized its details, and recalled the command from Carlos to destroy it. He would throw the pieces to the wind and they would scatter like white moths. But recalling the actions of Domingo, the ex-priest, Sandro popped the map into his mouth, chewed it and gulped it down, as if swallowing the entire landscape.

Dear Teresa,

I travel on and on, under sun and stars, across dry plateaus and over bare hills of bone. Why is it I feel, perhaps foolishly, I am coming nearer to you and not moving farther away?

I feel this journey is changing me, in ways I cannot explain. I am much surer of myself. I know what I am doing is right. I begin to wonder who I will be by the time I reach home. What kind of man will I have become?

We spent so little time together, you hardly had a chance to note my flaws, of which there are many, I must warn you. For one thing, I believe I am an unredeemed pagan, perhaps a mystic. Pagano y místico. I can only speak of these things to you, for we are of a new world. Even my family would not understand.

Teresa, this journey is a wonder to me, as are you.

Until then,
Sandro

§

Police Inspector Gonzalo Gonzalez y Alonso held before him a telegram from the offices of the Guardia Civil in Barcelona. He read from it as if it were an official declaration:

ARREST SANDRO RISCO CÁNOVAS - STOP - WANTED FOR GRAVE CRIMES IN BARCELONA - STOP - BELIEVED TO BE PART OF A VAST SOCIALIST CONSPIRACY DETERMINED TO UNDERMINE SPAIN - STOP - POSSIBLY BICYCLING ON THE ST JAMES WAY - STOP - LIKELY POSING AS A PILGRIM - STOP

The police inspector shook his head. "I had him — and let him go! *Mierda!* I was *that* close."

He paced up and down the knobby wooden-slatted floor of the post office, chewing at the corner of his moustache. "A famous criminal has passed through our town, *amigo*. He was here - with José, in the cathedral. And I let him escape!"

"How were you to know? You just received the telegram. They cannot blame you for that." The postmaster peered over his spectacles as he sorted letters.

"No, I suppose not." Gonzalo paused and looked at his friend. "But I must be the one to capture the scoundrel. It is my duty and I accept that duty."

"*Magnífico!*"

"First, I must think this through. I should place myself in the shoes of the criminal, to think as he would think." Gonzalo crumpled the telegram in his fist. "I must follow him on a bicycle myself! In that way I will be sure to choose the path he chooses."

"He would stay off the main roads, would he not?"

"Yes, I would think so, much of the time. Except for lonely stretches, of which there are many in Old Castile."

"But he has a head start."

"He cannot know I am following him and that is my great advantage."

"Perhaps he is just a *peregrino* after all."

"No, no — I recognize a criminal when I see one."

The postmaster nodded.

Gonzalo grew thoughtful. "Ferdinand, my friend, as you know I have no bicycle of my own. Might I use yours?"

"What? *Jamás.* I need it to deliver the mail, you know that."

"In these times, everyone must do their part. I will have to impound it if you do not lend it to me. Do you realize the paperwork involved? We would be wasting valuable time. The criminal is likely almost to Burgos by now. Your brother has a *bicicleta*. Use his while I am gone."

"All right. Fine. Take it, you *ladrón*. And good luck to you."

§

In late afternoon, the small, nearly enclosed square was cut by sunlight into the traditional halves of a bullring — *sol et sombra*. On the shady side sat two thin, wizened old men on spindly wooden chairs. In the dust at their feet snoozed a dog too lazy to bark at rare passersby.

Across from them, dressed entirely in black, a kerchief over her head, and sitting on a worn stone stoop under the full power of the sun, was an equally withered old woman.

They were so old they had grown immune to the passage of time. They watched with amazement as three bicycles in a single afternoon squeaked one by one into their village. The dog could not rouse itself to bark; it merely raised one pallid eyelid and returned to its nap.

As Sandro, the first arrival, came gasping into the almost-deserted village of San Juan de Ortega, he cut a woeful figure, covered head to foot in dust, rivulets of sweat leaving his face not unlike the twisted road he had just traveled.

One wrinkled old man asked the other, "*Mi hermano*, is it the Moors come back? Tell me. Is it? *Caramba!*"

The other man chomped his bare gums in reply.

Across the square, the old woman stood and shouted, "He has fallen in love with his revolver!" Sandro stared at her from a distance.

"Do not mind her. She is mad," said one of the men.

Sandro stopped and, holding Libertad, looked about the square lined with medieval stone buildings. "Where is everyone?"

"This is it," said one of the men from beneath his white moustache. "Everyone has gone except the priest and ourselves, two brothers and a wife, mine."

"Is she truly *loca?*"

"The sun's boiled her brains. She sits there and bakes."

She stood again, a wrinkled crow in a black shapeless dress, silver hair under the kerchief, and shouted across to them, "The future is the opiate of the young!"

Sandro shook his head and the two old men pointed out the priest's house where he could find food and shelter. The priest was always willing to assist pilgrims.

§

Meanwhile, Gonzalo struggled up a hill five kilometres from the same village. He had made tremendous gains in the past two days, exerting himself from dawn until dusk. Unfortunately, Ferdinand, who was a tiny man, owned a tiny bicycle. Gonzalo leaned over the handlebars, his massive shoulders, substantial moustache and fulsome head of heavily-oiled hair lending him the appearance of a beast, a bull or bison.

Twice Gonzalo had hit holes and tumbled to the ground. His right knee throbbed and his pant leg was ripped and flapped as he pumped. The little finger on his left hand, crumpled in the second fall, was surely broken for it, too, flashed with pain.

§

An hour behind Gonzalo came Ferdinand, pedaling like a maniac, his teeth clenched. In his pocket he carried a letter from Barcelona's chief of police addressed to Police Inspector Gonzalo Gonzalez y Alonso. The envelope was stamped PRIVADO! SECRETO! URGENTE! in red on both sides. Ferdinand felt that the letter, which had arrived a short while after the police inspector left, must be of sufficient importance to warrant hand delivery, so he borrowed his brother's bicycle and set off. He was sure he could catch the police inspector in a few short hours. He soon discovered he was wrong. Already it was late in the afternoon of his second day on the road. The sun was beginning to set.

§

Padre Mirlo had a kind and fatherly face and Sandro took an immediate liking to him. His long black cassock swirled around him as he busied himself gathering bread, cheese, sausage and several slices of *jamón*. He squatted to fill a jug of wine from a barrel in the corner.

"So, bicycling all the way to Santiago de Compostela, are you? In these times, imagine that." He came to the table with two earthenware cups and filled them from the jug.

"Has there been any fighting around here?"

"No, not yet." The padre wiped his mouth with his sleeve and refilled his cup.

They ate heartily and quickly. The wooden ceiling beams were hung, like a fat-encrusted cave, with *chorizo* sausages, once a hex against pork-fearing Moors, but now a quaint tradition.

Through an iron grille in the wall, they could hear the voice of the madwoman shouting on the plaza, "We must make the most of this triumph!"

This exclamation was prompted by the alarming arrival of Gonzalo. A stone had planted itself in his way, the tire had twisted, the bicycle had wobbled, he had slammed on the brakes and then he had gone flying over the handlebars into an inconvenient stone wall. Blood dripped from his forehead and lip and he held a tooth in the palm of his hand.

Before he could say anything, the two old men pointed and said, "The priest lives there. He will take care of you."

As he picked up the crumpled bicycle and made his way to the priest's house, the madwoman shouted after him: "Someone should finish off these swine bourgeois!"

Sandro was in the midst of gulping down his supper when there was a heavy knock at the door. The priest rose and went to answer it.

"Lord, what have we here? Come in, my son, come in."

Gonzalo and Sandro locked eyes. They gazed at each other for a moment in silence. Sandro swallowed.

The Inspector pointed and announced, "Sandro Risco Cánovas, I, Gonzalo Gonzalez y Alonso, Supreme Police Inspector for Santo Domingo de la Calzada, by the authority vested in me by the Supreme Police Authority of the region of Rioja," (*for God's sake, get on with it*, Sandro uttered *sotto voce*) "place you under arrest."

A half hour later they still sat around the table, arguing over cups of wine that had been filled and emptied half a dozen times.

"How could this be?" Padre Mirlo was incredulous and red-faced. "I know this boy. He could not do such a thing."

"You know him? How long have you known him, Padre?"

"But several hours and yet I hasten to add I am a distinguished judge of character. I have heard many confessions; this teaches one much about human nature."

"But Padre," the police inspector was losing patience, "the telegram said 'grave crimes,' so he must have murdered someone."

Sandro shook his head. "I did nothing. I am innocent, an innocent pilgrim on his way to Santiago de Compostela. You have the wrong man."

"Is your name not Sandro Risco Cánovas?"

"Yes, it is."

"Then I have the right man."

"No, you have the right name but the wrong man."

"You twist words like a Jesuit."

"Please," the priest interrupted, "Inspector, I understand that you must fulfill your duty. You may lock Sandro up in one of my rooms for the night and in the morning ... we will discuss it with clear heads." He took the jug back to the barrel, squatted, filled it and returned. "In the meantime, let us have a little more wine."

A few minutes into the next jug there was another knock at the door.

"Enter," said Padre Mirlo.

In walked Ferdinand the postmaster. "An important letter came for you, Inspector. I have ridden for two days straight to catch you."

Outside, the madwoman in the square shouted, "The money commodity must be divisible at will!"

The police inspector ripped open the envelope and read it. He looked up at the expectant faces around him. "It says, 'In the case of Sandro Risco Cánovas, time is of the essence.' "

"That's all?" said the postmaster, his eyes huge with disbelief. He sat down, lowered his head and wept.

§

Later, from the fugue-like blackness of his makeshift cell, Sandro heard the madwoman's cries sounding with the regularity of a chorus in a funeral oratorio:

"Individuals are slaves to the world market!"

"Culture began with Marx!"

"The only pure revolution is time!"

"Today's slogan is tomorrow's lyric!"

"The wild river despises all maps!"

Finally he slept. A short time later he felt a hand shake him awake, another hand over his mouth.

"Sandro, my son," the priest whispered, his breath smelling of onions and wine, "take these clothes and escape. The others are asleep. Go now. Go. Take the back road; you can't circle the square, the old lady will make a ruckus. Should you find yourself in León, head to the cathedral in the city's heart and find a priest, Father Emilio, an old friend of mine, a bit of a simpleton but kind-hearted. He will help you, I am sure. Godspeed."

Sandro slipped out, found Libertad and changed into the clothes in the double-deep shadows behind the church. *Has he given me a dress to wear? Am I to go the rest of the way disguised as a woman?*

It was not until dawn that he saw he had donned the robes of a priest.

§

In early morning, near an orchard, a truck stopped.

"Padre, will you bless our soldiers?"

Sandro halted and stood by the bicycle, trying to disguise his unease. He set the bicycle aside as a dozen soldiers climbed down from the back of the truck and knelt before him in the road. Sandro knew that if he mumbled in Latin no one would have the temerity to question the blessing.

Moving his right hand in the shape of a cross, index and middle finger extended, he said, "*In domino nomini patre filio et spirito*. Go in peace." He smiled indulgently and realized he had rather enjoyed it, this magnanimous gesture.

One *soldado*, older than the others, came over to him. "I, too, had a Star bicycle once. What will you do if you run into the Reds?"

"Bless them, I suppose."

"Hah. Bless them with a revolver, I say."

Sandro frowned. As a priest he was an even more visible target.

§

After persistently questioning Padre Mirlo, the inspector learned that Sandro was now impersonating a priest. He relayed this information to the Guardia Civil detachment in Burgos by telegram. Burgos was a city filled with priests, many of them at any one time on bicycles. Thus it was that seventeen priests, including a half dozen Franciscans, two Benedictines, an outraged beak-nosed Jesuit and even a nun, mistakenly rounded up in the confusion, spent the night in the Burgos jail. The jailer, still wrestling with the legacy of his education by the Jesuits, would not let the lone Jesuit go until he had memorized eighty lines of verse on sensual love by the medieval poet and archpriest Juan Ruiz.

Meanwhile, Sandro gave Burgos a wide berth and rode instead to the west, the police inspector a half day behind.

The moon, a ripe Valencia orange, guided Sandro through the warm and sensual dark. He thought of Teresa and breathed the night air deeply.

He rode on in silence but for the hiss of the tires along the empty, shining road.

§

"Have I not seen you at the Café Zona?"

The military officer addressing Teresa walked up to her as she stood in the thin shade by a stone wall, gazing over Barcelona from the high park of Tibidabo. They stood above the city, the sea shining to the east. Nearby, an amusement park rang with the clamour of excited voices and beside it a towering statue of Christ overlooked the city: palm, orange and plane trees along the boulevards and in the courtyards; new lines of apartment buildings and the jumble of ancient structures in the old quarters; the blunt fingers of the docks reaching into the Mediterranean.

"Sunday, I take it, is your day off?"

"Sí." She recognized him — one of the officers who sat at a table at the back of the café, the good-looking one with the blue-grey eyes. "I come here to get away." She tried to sound friendly, but uninterested.

"They say everyone in Barcelona these days is either a soldier, a thief or a spy. Which are you?"

"It's just an expression. It means nothing."

"Perhaps. Look, I am not here to play games. I know you have been listening to our conversations at the café. Probably reporting them to the anarchists or the Reds. Do you think I'm stupid? As you have been watching us, I have been watching you. I see you approach our table when the conversation turns serious, offering another glass of beer to patrons whose glasses are still half full. I made a few inquiries. Your barman has been arrested. I could have you arrested, too, in a minute."

She turned and looked at him. "What is it you want?"

"One week with you." He gazed at her.

She ran her hand through her hair. "Well, I'm honoured. An officer, no less."

"One week. After that, I can get you what you want. I can get you out of here. Your little revolution won't mean a thing. I could get you safe passage to the border, to France."

"If I wanted to go to France, which I don't, I could get there myself."

"Don't be so sure."

She turned back to the view. "Could you get me to the north coast, near Gijón?"

"Difficult, but possible. Why?"

"Tomorrow night then, after work, meet me a block east of the café."

"Good. Until then, *adiós*."

She watched him as he walked away, his broad shoulders, his confident gait. She shuddered at the sound of thunder, shivered at the first spattering of rain, fat drops presaging a deluge.

She lay awake on the floor that night while Jorge slept in her bed. He could now move about with the help of a crutch and could soon move to another apartment, stay with a friend in POUM. She could leave the city, though it was more difficult than she let on to the officer, and dangerous. She tossed and turned.

Jorge spoke from the bedroom. "Teresa, are you awake? What's wrong?"

"Nothing. Go back to sleep. You were dreaming."

§

The next day, she walked slowly to work. *She would faint. Fake an illness. Find some way out.* The café was filled with patrons. Above the bar hung dozens of fat bronzed hams, some with bits of hair and skin still attached. In clusters of three and four, soldiers stood chattering at the bar as they drank beer and sampled the tapas of olives, garlic potatoes and tortillas laid out on platters. The officer she expected had not yet arrived despite the fact that all of his friends sat at their usual table.

She served four glasses of inexpensive Carlos III brandy to the other officers at his table. "Isn't someone missing tonight?"

The officers glanced warily at each other, until one with a close-clipped moustache said, "Last night he was given a special assignment. But what business is it of yours? Asking questions only invites trouble."

She turned away. *She knew what 'special assignment' meant. Arrested.*

Late that night, she took a bottle of brandy home and celebrated with Jorge by getting joyously drunk.

§

The landscape was nothing but light itself. Brilliant and burning, it leached all colour from earth and sky. Every hill, stone and tree was infused with the chalk dust of light, too hot to touch, too hot to breathe.

In each town and village, the inevitable stone church provided Sandro a blessedly cool sanctuary, a place to sit for a few moments out of the sun. Sandro took more than one siesta lolling in a back pew.

In the heat of a late morning, he entered a small village, saw a church on a square and headed straight for it.

Mass was in progress. Holding the door half open, he hesitated before taking a seat at the back to avoid drawing attention to himself. The first five or six pews were filled with old women, dressed from head to foot in black, and a few white-haired men. The rest of the church was empty. He leaned back in the cool dark and drifted on the familiar Latin intonations.

A hefty priest hoisted himself up the stone stairs to the pulpit to deliver the gospel and sermon. He disappeared for a moment in the spiraling stairwell and then reappeared in the pulpit. Carefully, he removed a scarlet ribbon from the Bible and read from the Gospel of Matthew.

Sandro moved a few pews closer to listen. The door at the rear of the church swung wide. No one else noticed, but Sandro watched with curiosity as a man with a sharp black beard entered, bearing what appeared to be two long sticks. The young man stood the poles on end and deftly mounted a pair of stilts. He strutted down the main aisle, a bizarre long-legged insect.

By this time the rest of the congregation had seen him approach; he was now on the same level as the priest in his pulpit.

Three metres from the pulpit, the man halted and shouted at the priest: "*Hipócrita!* You gaze down on these people from your place of eminence, terrifying them with fear of eternal damnation, forcing your ideas down their throats, keeping them in poverty, while you live like a king!"

The priest threw up his hands. "Enough, Luis. *Váyase!* Get out!"

The worshippers began to whisper. Three women stood and walked toward the stilt-walker, their baggy black stockings gathered around their heavy shoes. One raised her fist and swore at him, another shook his stilts. He stepped closer to the priest, hopped off the stilts and hung from the edge of the pulpit. The priest took this opportunity to close his Bible and use it to pound the poor wretch's knuckles.

"*Demonio! Comunista!*"

"I am an anarchist, not a Red!" Luis shouted back.

"Someone get the Guardia!" a matronly woman cried. An old man limped toward a side door. A crowd milled about below the pulpit. One elderly woman had hold of a stilt and was poking Luis from below.

Believing that the anarchist was about to be murdered on the spot, Sandro could not help crying out, "Stop! Leave him be!"

At this the crowd turned and looked at Sandro and some, seeing he was a priest, hesitated. Others, however, taking him to be an accomplice of the anarchist and perhaps a renegade priest to boot, gave chase. The officiating priest hurried down the stairs of the pulpit, cassock flying.

Sandro ran for the door and, like a trumpet blast, the light and heat hit him full in the face. He fled down the church steps, hopped on Libertad and pedaled hard down the street. The crowd shouted obscenities after him and shook their fists. An old wrinkled *yaya* with a stilt still in hand flung it with surprising vigour across the square.

§

The bicycle skidded through a patch of gravel as Sandro reached the bottom of a hill where a nearly dry *arroyo* ran through a narrow canyon. The thin waterway was lined with low trees and brush. He pumped hard through the pedal-high grass. Stashing Libertad in the bushes, he climbed a short way up the hill and stumbled behind a cluster of hazelnut trees. From this vantage he looked down the road to the bottom of the hill. His breath came hard and fast, sweat stung his eyes.

Clickity-click. Clickity-click. The police inspector skittered down the hill, sliding in the gravel, his coat flying out behind him. He was intent on building speed to take a run at the next long hill looming ahead. Sandro held his breath until the inspector crested the hill, followed the road along the ridge, then dipped from sight.

He is too persistent, this one. I must take care. Sandro lay back, closed his eyes and was asleep in moments.

When he awoke, he had to fix a flat tire, the third that week. As he worked, he saw a line of penitents climbing the hill following a rutted cart track speckled with grey-white pebbles. When they had disappeared he rode in the other direction until he saw a small church on a low bare hill, its buff stone the same colour as the distant fields.

He pedaled slowly toward the church and a lone chestnut tree next to it. A man sat in the shade on a stone slab bench, reading a newspaper. Roped to the tree was a patient donkey, one perky ear and one ear shriveled like a dried leaf.

"*Hola.*"

"*Hola,*" returned the reader from behind the paper.

"The chapel, is it open?"

Still the man did not lower the paper. Sandro noted his clean fingernails and shiny shoes.

"It is no longer a chapel, but a museum and, yes, it is *abierto.*"

Sandro turned and looked about. There was nothing else around. He was sure he was the only visitor this lonely site would receive today and yet the man ignored him.

Sandro turned back to the reader, who was still holding his paper high. "Politics?"

"*Sí.*"

Sandro nodded, leaned the bicycle against the wall and entered the museum.

The cool interior was nearly empty but for a glass case, like an altar, in the middle of the room and a single broom standing in the corner. Inside the case was a book, lying open to a page about half way through. Sandro leaned over. It was a map of a portion of the pilgrimage route to Santiago. As far as he could tell, the map depicted, in dusty colours of gold, blue and madder, a portion of the road that passed nearby. To the right, the road split into two routes that ended at the edge of the page: these were labeled THE WAY OF DIFFICULTY and THE WAY OF EASE. Inspecting the case, he found that it was locked securely with a rusty padlock that dangled from the right corner. He let its cold weight rest in his hand.

"May I be of assistance?" The man stood in the doorway, watching Sandro warily. The keeper was jauntily dressed in a white shirt, black tie and formal jacket.

"Would it be possible to turn the page?"

"*Por qué?*"

Sandro paused. "It seems to me that if one is to display a book that reveals only a single page, one merely draws attention to the fact that the majority of what could be seen remains invisible."

"You have a point. I will fetch the key."

He disappeared into a back room and reappeared a moment later. "The key is not on its hook." He shrugged.

Sandro waited. When no more information was forthcoming, he said, "Could someone else perhaps have the key?"

"Ah." He pointed at the broom in the corner. "Perhaps *la señora* Riaz who comes to clean. I will see."

The man untied the donkey, mounted and rode bumpily down the hill. Sandro sat on the bench in the shade and read the newspaper. Half an hour later the man returned, slid off the donkey and announced, "*La señora* Riaz does not have the key. She thinks perhaps the priest in Burgos has it."

"Burgos!" Sandro shook his head. "How inconvenient." Returning to the case, Sandro took the lock in his hand and gave it a good tug, fully expecting it to fall open.

The man stood in the doorway behind him. "*Señor*, please do not attempt force."

"You do not understand." Sandro pointed through the glass. "The book shows a small portion of the Camino Real but then, you see, it splits, and I do not know where it goes."

"I see. Then the road is like life, yes? We do not know where we have come from, nor do we know where we are going. Displaying a single page makes a peculiar kind of sense, does it not? But enough of *filosofía*. Please join me for coffee. I am about to make fritters from an excellent recipe I found in the newspaper some months ago. We will have a good discussion about politics."

My dear Teresa,

So much has happened. It appears I have taken vows. I wear a priest's robes now. They are really rather comfortable, though they do make it more difficult to pedal.

I am blistered and blackened by the sun. When I ride by day, my hair grows too hot to touch. Sometimes I wrap a shirt around my head and look like an Arab. Indeed, it is a kind of Sahara I am crossing. Yesterday afternoon, while everyone slept through their siesta, I rode along a dirt track in low dusty hills. No shade in any direction. I felt I was about to burst into flames, trailing fire as I sailed through the hot afternoon light.

I believe that at the end of my road somehow you will be there, that I will have come full circle.

In so many ways, I am burning.

Until then,
Sandro

§

Sandro hopped off the bicycle and stared. A tall blond-haired man ran toward him, his backpack bouncing, his hands waving in the air.

"Into the trees! *Vamos!*" he shouted. "They're coming! They're coming!"

Sandro had no idea what he was talking about, but hid Libertad in the thick brush before following the man to the foot of a towering beech tree.

"*Quién?*" Sandro asked.

"Guardias. Up, up."

"Did they see you?"

"No. I don't think so."

The two men threaded up through the limbs, climbing higher and higher into a tangle of leaves, thick branches and twigs. At last they reached a place where two large limbs diverged almost horizontally from the main trunk. They sat, straddling the smooth grey bark twenty metres above the forest floor.

Through the thicket of leaves, they glimpsed several Guardias marching along the road. Two peasant prisoners, with their hands tied behind their backs, walked ahead of them. A wheezy truck stuttered behind. Thirty metres past the beech, they stopped and prepared to make camp by a stream.

"*Mierda!*" said Sandro's new companion. "They're halting."

"*Gracias.* For the warning, I mean."

"No trouble." He held out his hand. "Adam. Adam Weatherhead."

"I am Sandro Risco Cánovas. Where are you from?"

"You mean Padre Sandro, don't you?" Adam eyed Sandro's cassock.

"Well, yes."

"Canada."

Sandro nodded. "What are you doing in our country?"

"I've come to learn what I can about the Spanish *Revolución*. But all the talk in Barcelona was getting me down. Nobody was doing anything but arguing. I probably shouldn't be saying this to a priest. But I know you're no priest, are you?"

Sandro did not reply, returning his gaze instead to the Guardias below. "I think they are planning to spend the night."

"Good thing they camped by that noisy stream. We could be shouting and they wouldn't hear us."

"It is a comfortable tree. And I have a supply of food."

Adam patted his knapsack. "I've plenty of food and water, as well."

Neither Sandro nor Adam wanted to risk climbing down until the Guardias left. Even if they tried to escape at night, their movements might disturb the dogs in the nearby village. So they stayed put, talking, reading, eating. They slept embracing the tree's main trunk and stuck leaves in their clothes for camouflage. They were sure they were invisible high in the chiaroscuro of the forest.

That first night Sandro was awakened five times by loud snoring. He reached around the trunk and shook Adam by the shoulder.

In the morning, Sandro said bluntly, "You snore."

"No, I don't."

"I had to shake you so the Guardias would not hear."

The sun trickling down through the leaves patterned their hands and faces.

Each breeze set the forest shivering, a wave of sunlit green shards in the willows on the edge of the forest, a slow sough of wind through slim, flickering leaves. The breeze advanced, washing through pines, leathery oaks and finally their own stand of beech. Each type of leaf made its own distinctive sound.

Adam picked his teeth with a twig and looked at Sandro from around the tree trunk. "So, you said last night you don't believe in the Revolution. You're a priest but you ran when the Guardias came. Why?"

"Yes, well, everyone wants you to choose a side, do they not? But I do not care to choose sides. Anyway, the Guardias will shoot before you can answer their questions."

"They wouldn't shoot a priest. Anyway, it was a mess in Barcelona — splinter groups splintering off other splinter groups. I'm a member of POUM myself." Adam shrugged. "So, where are you coming from?"

"I, too, am coming from Barcelona. I am a *peregrino*, following the Saint James Way to Santiago de Compostela."

"A pilgrim? In these times?"

"I know, I know. But I have met a few other pilgrims crazy enough to travel these days; also a few gypsies, a rope-maker and a troublesome policeman who may or may not still be following me. I am from a little village called Arcasella on the Sea of Cantabria. My father was a poor fisherman, but I was a good student so the priest convinced a rich man formerly from our village to fund my education. I studied engineering in Barcelona."

"An engineer? Not a priest? Why did you go to school in Barcelona? Why not closer to home?"

"My uncle, my mother's brother, was in the navy and settled in Barcelona. When I was a child he was always kind to me. We were very close. He told my parents to send me to Barcelona and he would keep an eye on me."

"Did he?"

"Of course not. He introduced me to all the best drinking establishments in the city. But he is a good-hearted man. Always slipping me money, although he is often away at sea."

"What happened? You become a priest instead of an engineer?"

"No, not exactly. I met an archaeology professor who needed two drafting students to work for him. Professor Gomez offered the job to my friend Jorge and myself. We spent the summer working in the caves in the foothills near Altamira, a little west of Santander. Have you heard of Altamira?"

"I think so."

"In many caves in France and Spain, like those in Altamira and those where we worked at Linares, there are ancient wall paintings — mostly mammals of different sorts: bison, bulls, ibexes, horses, deer. And handprints."

Adam glanced up at a goldfinch that landed nearby. "Any paintings of birds?"

"No. It is strange, but there are few birds. Almost all are of mammals, a few fish. The paintings are tens of thousands of years old. Much of the work is very beautiful, as fine as the work of the artists of the Renaissance, although I am no expert. I spent a summer lying on my back sketching for the professor, numbering artifacts, small statues and so on. It was fascinating work so I decided to become an archaeologist. And, no, I am not really a priest."

"And your village, the priest, your parents — what do they think of this?"

"The priest believes I will come to my senses. But they don't understand." Sandro yawned. "And you?"

"I studied Classics at Cambridge and Toronto. But I was tired of history and theory and wanted a taste of the real world, the modern world. I decided to come here — the Left needs our help."

"Perhaps you are really a spy."

"You're the one wearing a disguise. I could tell the moment I looked at you, you're not a man of the cloth. Anyway, it doesn't matter. As for my story, the less you know, the better."

The sun set and Adam pulled some apples, cheese and bread from his pack. The air cooled. As they ate, smells of beans and sausage drifted up to them from the Guardia camp.

Sandro told Adam about Jorge and Teresa, the fateful night Jorge was shot and the events of his last few days in Barcelona. Finally they prepared for sleep. They decided to use Sandro's rope to tie themselves to the tree trunk so they wouldn't fall during the night. They wrapped themselves in blankets, leaned forward against the trunk and slept.

"Maybe the Guardias will leave tomorrow."

§

The damp morning began, as usual, with birdsong. As Adam and Sandro ate their breakfast bread and a handful of walnuts, they could hear the Guardias below, rising and going through their morning ablutions while smoke from cooking fires drifted skyward. After a while, the truck headed down the road and through the village. Adam and Sandro listened closely. A small contingent of the Guardias had been left behind to watch the prisoners.

"About those caves you mentioned," Adam said. "When were they first found?"

"In the 1870s. At first, no one believed they were authentic. Most agreed that the paintings had been faked. Marcelino de Sautuola found the paintings at Altamira in 1879, I believe."

"Who was he?"

"An amateur archaeologist. He was searching for artifacts near the entrance to the cave. When his five-year-old daughter wandered into the cave with her lamp, she noticed the paintings of bulls on the ceiling and came running out to tell her father. Once he inspected the paintings, he reported his discovery, but the experts called him a liar and insisted the paintings were faked. Though more and more painted caves were found over the next thirty years in France and Spain, experts thought one fraud had merely spawned others. You see, there was no easy way to verify their authenticity." Sandro paused on hearing voices in the camp below. He peeked between the branches at the road. "*Mierda*! It is him!"

"Who?"

"The policeman who has been following me. *Maldita sea*!"

A Guardia spoke with the police inspector and shook his head while the inspector leaned against his bicycle. After several minutes he rode off.

Sandro took a slow drink of water, his eyes closed.

"Go ahead," Adam urged him, "I'd like to hear more."

"Yes, of course. When I saw the *pueblo* of Altamira, I noticed that the professors and curious travelers who had come to visit the caves were wealthy. Since they had to stay in the *pueblo* to be near the caves, the villagers suddenly had more money than they had ever had in their lives. Before the discovery of the caves, even Altamira had been as poor as my own village."

Adam rubbed his chin. "Could someone live in those caves?"

"No. They have too many visitors. But other caves might be all right. *Gitanos* sometimes live in caves up north. At Linares, where I worked, we searched in nearby foothills for new cave sites with a couple of village men. We blew narrow openings with small charges of dynamite. They taught Jorge and me how to set the dynamite ourselves. We did find a few small caves, but no paintings."

A flock of blackbirds landed noisily in the surrounding trees and raised a ruckus. Morning had passed into afternoon. Sandro yawned. A meandering breeze shifted the leaves. Two Guardias argued over a card game.

"How old did you say those paintings were?"

"They vary. Some are almost twenty-five thousand years old."
Adam shook his head. "*Increíble.*"

"By the turn of the century, the pendulum had swung the other way. So many painted caves were discovered that the experts were forced to change their minds. Dozens of new sites were found and studied. There was no doubt they were genuine."

Sandro reached for a piece of cheese from his bag resting on an upper branch. In an instant he was flailing through branches, tumbling down and down before landing on a large branch that broke his fall. The breath had been knocked out of him and he lay on his stomach, his chest aching.

Adam stood high above, whispering, "Are you all right? Sandro? Sandro?"

Sandro couldn't answer, but hoped Adam would hear the three Guardias approaching the tree. "*Hola.* Who goes there?" they shouted.

Adam was silent and Sandro tried not to move. A sudden shot made Sandro twitch and sent a half dozen birds soaring into the sky. A bullet ripped through leaves several trees away. More random shots followed. Sandro closed his eyes and prayed he wouldn't fall farther. A trickle of sweat ran into his eyes. One more shot, closer this time, splintered a nearby branch.

The shooting stopped as the old truck coughed up the road toward the guards. It halted and a chorus of voices shouted, "We have girls and *vino! Vamos, vamos!*"

The Guardias hurried to join their friends, saying they had heard a bear in the trees and the others laughed.

Sandro tried moving his fingers, one at a time. His chest hurt badly and he was afraid to move for fear of falling farther. "Adam, the rope. Bring the rope."

In a moment Adam was next to him, the rope looped over his arm. "Tie it around my waist," said Sandro.

Adam quickly tied the knot and secured the other end of the rope to a sturdy branch. He gave the rope a tug. Sandro backed up slowly, shifting his weight only after testing each movement. Suddenly his left leg fell through the tangle of small branches and he hung upside down, facing the trunk of the tree.

"I think I might have broken a rib," Sandro said after he had righted himself with Adam's help. He held his hand over his chest and tried to keep his breathing shallow. "I'm dizzy."

"Wait here. Rest." Adam scrambled up through the tree and scuttled back down with the water.

"We've got to get out of here. Maybe tonight. What do you think?"

"Not yet. I am not sure I can run."

"Can you climb?"

"I'll try."

Sandro took an excruciating thirty minutes to climb back up, stopping often. "From now on, we stay tied in place all the time, night and day," Adam said.

§

The next morning, the Guardias slept late, hung over no doubt, although there was at least one guard awake to watch over the prisoners.

Adam leaned forward and whispered hoarsely. "Tell me more about the caves. Were there caves in your own village?"

"When I was young, I found a cave in a forest not far from my village. I used to go there to be alone. Only Pedro and I knew about it. We told no one." Sandro shifted his position. "*Ay! Ay!*" He paused to get comfortable again.

"When I worked for the professor in Linares, I was amazed by the sheer number of paintings: horses, bulls, bison, deer, all sorts of geometric shapes, clusters of dots, handprints. I spent days alone with my *lámpara* and sketchbook. I dug for sculptures and artifacts in the soil under the paintings. There was something about the place. At night, I would close my eyes and watch the animals gather and swirl. I could see the beasts on the insides of my eyelids, passing in and out of each other, overlapping, running, alive. I could feel them breathing inside me."

§

Late-afternoon light tilted through the trees. Sandro finished writing the letter he had been leaning over for the past half hour and put it in his bag with the others. Adam peeled the prickly covering off a beechnut. He popped the nut in his mouth and took another swig of wine from the wineskin.

"Didn't it feel like a bloody tomb sometimes, in that cave all day, just you and the silence?"

"Yes, but in a way it was also a mouth, speaking from somewhere deep in the past. Those artists were communicating with their future, with us. It was there that I planned ... but never mind."

Adam drank deeply, only half-listening, involved in drunken musings of his own.

"Imagine being the first humans to create an image of a bull. They must have felt like gods, shaping beasts from the earth. And handprints. Their own hands, their signatures." Sandro looked at his palm, its lines like roads through low hills.

Adam lifted the wineskin to his lips. "*In vino veritas.*"

§

The next morning began with a fine drizzle. By midday, the wind charged through the leaves and branches, driving the rain horizontal. They were soaked and miserable.

Adam's eyes appeared dark, his lids heavy. He could feel rainwater running off his own hair and down the back of his neck.

"I am so damnably stiff." Adam rubbed his knees. "I must get down. A fellow could go mad up here. Do you think we could make it?"

"No. It is too dangerous."

The sky darkened and lightning split the heavens, twining down among the beeches and oaks and willows like upended forests of light.

Adam ran his hands through his hair, twisting his head from side to side. He was shaking. Thunder rumbled nearby. Wind blasted through the trees. Adam looked wild. He took his first step down.

Sandro grabbed the front of Adam's shirt in his fist, pulled him up and slapped him hard in the face. Adam stopped, stunned, and leaned his head against the trunk of the tree and closed his eyes.

After a while, the dripping was punctuated only by the rumbles of distant thunder. They sat in silence as the storm dissipated to a faint murmur.

"Are you all right?"

"Yes. I am … I am … well, somewhat embarrassed. I believe I lost control of my senses for a moment."

Sandro strained to see through the branches. "Perhaps they will leave tomorrow."

§

A shot ruptured the dawn's silence. Sandro and Adam bolted awake and stared at each other.

Adam stood and tried to see through the branches. "Peasants with rifles, on the road. They are trying to rescue the prisoners. Can you run?"

Sandro nodded. He untied the rope and, moving gingerly, started the descent.

"How are your ribs? Let me help you." Adam reached out.

In moments they were on the ground. Sandro grabbed Libertad out of the brush and ran into the forest, Adam close behind. Soon they came to a cattle path that led to a rutted road.

Adam stopped. "Ride on, *padre peregrino*. I will merely slow you down now. Godspeed, and if I am ever in Arcasella I will look you up."

"Adam, would you do me a favour? When you return to Barcelona, would you deliver these letters for me?" Sandro pulled the bundle from his bag and handed it to Adam. "Deliver it personally. To Teresa Maza. San Miguel, number 5. Do not forget, but please do *not* write down the address. San Miguel, number 5. You will do this for me?"

"Yes, of course." Adam took the packet and placed it in his knapsack.

Sandro clasped his hand. "Thank you, for everything. *Buena suerte! Adiós.*"

"Good luck, until we meet again."

Sandro rode on, taking his secret with him.

Dearest Teresa,

I am sitting in a tree to write you this letter. I have been almost a week living in the branches of a beech with a friend from Canada, Adam Weatherhead. I will ask him to deliver this and my other letters to you when we leave, for he is heading back to Barcelona. There are times when I think we have both gone mad. I fell once and thought I had broken a rib. I have been forced to hide as we are very near a Guardia encampment. They are oblivious to us, but we are trapped. We will have to choose our moment of escape carefully.

I believe the streets of Barcelona are shining as you walk about the city. Know that I think of you constantly.

Until then,

Sandro

§

In the middle of the afternoon, in the middle of nowhere, Sandro came upon a dead man sprawled in the road. He stopped and hopped off his bicycle, setting it down gently.

"He's dead. Don't touch him, Padre."

The voice came from Sandro's right. A peasant sat on a stone in the shade of an elm tree, smoking a cigarette. He had deep wrinkles, his face like tanned hide.

"*Mi hermano.*"

Sandro nodded and looked at the dead man who was lying on his back, his legs splayed, a patch of blood, in the pattern of an oak leaf, on his shirtfront. A fat bluebottle fly landed on his cheek. Sandro wanted to swish it away, but didn't. The fly crawled into the man's nostril, then flew out a moment later.

"What happened?"

"I found him this way. An hour ago, maybe two."

"We should move him off the road."

"Do not touch him."

"We cannot leave him here. What if someone comes?"

The peasant turned and stared at Sandro as if he were an apparition. An uncomfortable silence followed. The fly landed again on the man's face, fretted over the corpse's cheek and lips. That the man could not wave it away was the surest sign that he was dead.

"He should be buried. I will help you. Do you have a shovel?"

"Why? Let the sun eat him."

Sandro looked down the road, hoping to see the approach of a farmer's cart or a donkey, someone to help.

"Go about your business, Padre. You are no help here. Though you could bless him."

Sandro went through the motions, making the sign of the cross and saying a few mumbled prayers over the corpse. The peasant said nothing, but dismissed him with a wave of the hand.

§

Sun and earth; hammer and anvil. The long strokes of sunlight pound down from the sky, the heat a kind of weight, slams against the unyielding, hard-packed dust. He rides on, pumping through stone and light.

He sleeps, troubled and sweaty, for an hour in the shade of an oak tree. As he rises and steps out of the shade, the light hits him like a silent explosion. He decides he must bicycle during siesta when the world is empty and he is sure he will meet no one on the road.

The pressure of light bangs on his head. The hot dry air penetrates his clothes, crackling and lifting another layer of his skin, as if he were a martyr at the mercy of a thousand bright knives.

The world sleeps, hidden from the violence of light, in some dark cool place and yet he must ride on, drive on, forever. Sweat flows from him, trickles down his neck, out of his ears, down his forehead and into his eyes, running in a steady stream off the end of his nose, over his upper lip and into his mouth. It runs down his spine and into the crack of his ass, splits into two rivulets to continue coursing down his legs, inside his knees. It collects in his shoes, rimed with salt and uneven white stains.

Shade and light. He believes they are the two sides of the same political argument. As one moves forward, the other retreats, two armies pushing against each other, one laying claim to three metres of dusty, useless terrain, until the other pushes forward and retakes it. Light and shade. The one can never inhabit the other's world. They destroy each other. Is it their nature? Must it be?

§

In the evening, Sandro had a few walnuts, some half-stale bread and water.

"Grawk!" a crow greeted him from a nearby tree. When he mounted Libertad in the dusk and started to pedal, the bird swept down and perched atop Sandro's small suitcase. *An ally, perhaps.*

Sandro and Libertad slalomed down a long hill in the twilight. The crow flew off and soared ahead of them. After Sandro took a wide, slow curve, the bird settled back into place.

"I do believe we have made a friend, Libertad." Sandro would name the crow Puntillo da Parrapunte after a captain of the Knights Templar, whose seal depicted two riders on a single horse.

§

Puntillo da Parrapunte became Sandro's constant companion. Sometimes he would fly away and disappear for a few hours, but he always returned to his perch on the back of the bicycle. If the truth were told, Sandro was happy for the company, such as it was. Suddenly it seemed Libertad flew with greater ease over the hills and plains.

One evening toward dusk, storm clouds towered in the west, upside-down mountains of grey, turning purple in the lower reaches, then black in the hanging tips. The tickle of a breeze grew forceful and kicked up the fields in sporadic gusts. Sandro stretched forward, stood on the pedals and pumped hard, toward a small abandoned hut in the distance. The air began to darken and lightning flickered across the flat fields.

As he jumped from the bike and entered the hut, the crow leapt into a leafless tree nearby, tucked his head under his wing and fell asleep, the wind riffling through his feathers.

§

A toothless flower merchant handed Teresa her bouquet with a gracious smile. She knew this old man with liver spots on his hands; he stole flowers from the cemetery by night and sold them on the street by day. It was a story that stayed among the poor and never reached the ears of the bourgeoisie. The old man was able to keep himself in bread and wine, though little else.

Teresa walked along the Ramblas and found an empty bench. Too often lately, when delivering messages to the captain of her revolutionary cell — snatches of conversation she overheard in the café, numbers and movements of soldiers — she had felt a tingling on the back of her neck. Someone was watching her.

Men and women walked by, the usual parade of daily life: students, businessmen, soldiers, mothers with toddlers, gypsies, Guardia Civil in tri-cornered patent-leather hats.

She took a cheap book from her bag and began reading. The book was a romance in which she had no interest at all, but it gave her the opportunity to glance up occasionally to see if anyone was watching her.

As she sat in the dappled shade, she remembered something Sandro had said to her in one of their all-night conversations before he left. He had been talking about the caves and compared them to the tree-lined tunnel of the Ramblas, the nearby buildings, the subway, people going in and out, everything enclosed and humming with energy. These city dwellers were like the animals on the cave walls, with their simple hungers and endless vitality, the way they spun through time, frenzied by needs and desires, constantly on the move. Yet ultimately they were caught in a terrible, constricted circle.

She noticed a man leaning against a tree, watching her, picking his teeth. *Too obvious. They are better than that, subtler, more discreet.*

§

Late that evening, Teresa sat at the kitchen table, writing while Jorge slept. She bent over the table, emptying her loneliness onto the page so Sandro might swallow it, make it disappear. She filled two sides of a sheet. Taking up the candle, she went to the window, open wide on the warm night. Holding the paper by one corner, she watched it leap into flame. A thin plume of smoke curled into the sky and disappeared to the west as the page dissolved into ash.

§

Jorge sat up in bed, the silence of mid-afternoon marred only by the scratching of his pencil and the occasional bell from a distant streetcar. Teresa sat across the room in a straight-backed chair, hands in lap. She was completely still, gazing up at a mirror on the wall.

He glanced at her, lowered his eyes to the page, glanced up again. He noted the cleft in her chin, the eyes as black as aubergines.

"I'm being followed."

"Turn your chin a little toward me." He paused, looked up, continued sketching. "By whom?"

"I'm not sure." She didn't look at him when she spoke. "Whoever it is, he isn't a professional."

"Professional?"

"Not the military. Not the police. I suspect it's one of our own on the left — CNT perhaps."

"Why would they want to follow you?"

"I don't know. But he's an amateur. I have no trouble losing him."

He paused to stretch and rub the back of his neck. "Perhaps you should stop for a while?"

"I can't. My work is too important."

"Ah, yes, the Revolution, the Revolution."

"Are you growing cynical now that you have regained your health?"

"No, merely impatient. I do not have your strength, your fortitude."

"So, let me see it."

Jorge handed her the drawing.

"It doesn't look like me in the least."

"I knew you would say that."

§

Sandro slept the night in the small, abandoned hut. Awakened early in the morning by the sound of bicycle tires on gravel, he glanced out the window. The police inspector dismounted.

"*Mierda*," breathed Sandro.

The inspector glanced up at the sky. In the same instant Puntillo da Parrapunte swept down from a branch to descend upon him, beating the air and pecking at his face. The crow attacked, flickered back up into the sky, only to attack again with redoubled ferocity. One pass raised a bloody streak on the inspector's forehead and face. When he touched the wound and saw his hand smeared with blood, the inspector leaped onto his bicycle and took off down the road toward León.

§

Sandro rode slowly that day, hoping the police inspector would have come and gone by the time he reached León.

As he rounded a curve, Sandro came face to face with a roadblock. *Do not run. Offer to bless them. Fascists, republicans, even anarchists will not refuse a blessing.* He drew close enough to make them out. *Guardias. Mierda.*

"Padre, how is it that you travel with a bird?" A Guardia Civil called to him as Sandro glided to a halt.

He was a young one, the worst kind, serious and by-the-book. Three other Guardia Civil stood next to a covered truck, smoking. The young one barked, "Where are you from? Where are you going? What's your business on this road? Open that bag."

With shaking hands, Sandro opened the suitcase and watched the guard root through it. He showed particular interest in the bag of pigments.

"What is this stuff? To make a bomb? Anybody could wear priest's clothes, even a *comunista*. What is it?" He held up the bag.

"Pigments. I paint. Scenes of the Camino Santiago."

"What do you paint *on*? Where are the canvases? And you're badly in need of a shave, Padre."

"I have a sketchbook here. See?" He held it up.

"Grawk!" said the crow and a heavyset older guard laughed heartily, removed his hat and wiped his sleeve across his forehead. The double row of his brass buttons glinted in the sun. "Greetings, Father, how are you today?"

"He's got a bag of chemicals, and he says he's a painter, but no canvas, no brushes," the young guard accused.

"I draw first." Sandro riffled through the pages for the older guard, who glanced at the book and then ignored it.

"These aren't dangerous chemicals. No explosives. Let him go." The older guard turned and walked back to the truck.

§

Sandro stood at the door of the cloister behind the cathedral in León, leaning against Libertad.

"Padre Emilio? I have been sent by Padre Mirlo, who says he is a friend of yours."

"Is that right? I see, of course. Sí, sí, come in, come in. We will put your *bicicleta* in the courtyard where it will be safe." He stopped short. "You have a bird on the back."

"Yes, a tame crow. He is no trouble."

The priest shrugged. He had one good eye, but his other swam about loosely in its socket, unhinged. Sandro found it disconcerting at first, but soon grew used to it.

"Have you eaten? You must be hungry, yes? We have a pot of stew and good dark bread."

Sandro sat at the wooden table in the simple refectory off the kitchen. Several other priests at the table ignored him or gave him a single, incurious glance and went back to their meals.

"Grawk!" sounded Puntillo in the courtyard.

Through the open door walked a grey-haired, distinguished-looking priest. He addressed Padre Emilio: "What is that bicycle doing in the courtyard and who is this?"

Emilio turned, "Padre Mateo, this is Padre Sandro. I have just heard he is riding his *bicicleta* along the pilgrim's route to Santiago."

"In these times? Astounding," the older priest said dryly. "See that he has a bed for the night and breakfast in the morning and then send him on his way. And get rid of that *cuervo*."

§

That night, Puntillo was left to fend for himself in the shed. He slept on an open beam above Libertad.

After everyone else had fallen asleep, Sandro sneaked down from his room to the kitchen. He filled a sack with three large dried sausages, bread, cheese, apples, oranges and pears. In the distance he heard rifle fire.

"What have you got there?"

Sandro spun around on hearing the accusing voice of Padre Mateo.

"Oh, Father, I am filling my sack for my pilgrim's journey."

"Why do you sneak about like a thief? We would have given you food. Come here. Sit down. I want to talk to you."

Sandro followed the priest back into the kitchen.

"Listen, my son. I know you are not a priest. No, no. Do not argue with me. You could be a *socialista*, a *comunista*, an anarchist, a common criminal, a fascist, who knows? You could be here to spy on us, to report us to the authorities. Though I do not know what your business is, I sense you are not a danger. Do not worry. I am not about to turn you in."

Sandro bowed his head. *"Muchas gracias."*

"But I am afraid you cannot stay here. Do not divulge your secrets to Padre Emilio. He is a good-hearted man, but will tell all he knows to any that ask, without understanding the problems he might cause. Continue to play the priest with him and the others. Take the food. If you are hungry, it is yours. But do not linger in León. Shall I give you my blessing?"

Sandro hesitated.

"I see. Let us at least shake hands. God go with you, my son."

§

The priests of the house were up early, already eating breakfast in the refectory by the time Sandro joined them.

"My apologies. I slept in. What a joy a bed is after weeks on the road."

"Your pilgrim's travels must exhaust you," said Padre Emilio. "Before breakfast, would you like to say Mass? We have extra vestments and I will attend you. I would be honoured."

"*Sí*, of course."

In the priests' personal chapel at the rear of the cloister, Sandro donned his vestments, Emilio handing them to him one by one. He thought he should kiss the soutane, or was it the surplice, before donning it. He was unsure, so he kissed all the garments. Emilio grinned.

Before donning the sleeveless chasuble, which went over the alb, Sandro paused to admire a scene of the Last Judgment on the back of the vestment.

Sandro strode to the altar and began by opening the large missal that sat on a lectern. The book, coppery with age and well-thumbed, fell open naturally at the canon of the Mass. Sandro began: "*Ad te levavi animam meam.* To you I have lifted up my soul ..." The memory of the ritual he had attended as a child came to him unbidden.

He turned the page and stared a moment at a depiction of the crucifixion. He remembered from the days he was an altar boy that the crucifix in the bottom right corner was meant to be kissed by the officiating priest. He did so.

He read from the gospel of Luke and when he was finished, Padre Emilio, who was serving, whispered, "You will please deliver a short sermon?" Sandro smiled and nodded. Emilio seated himself in the front pew, while Sandro took his place behind the pulpit.

"Today I would like to talk briefly about the life of a *peregrino.* I began my pilgrimage alone and I will no doubt finish alone. This has given me much time to reflect. I have, however, been attended by nature, God's greatest creation. It has been a time of simple miracles and ordinary joys. Though it has been a long journey, fraught with dangers and difficulties, these have passed. The long night comes to an end in a refreshing dawn. I give thanks for the possibility of making this pilgrimage. I cannot say it has been my life's dream, but having come this far I will not turn back. Thank you and God be with you. *Deo gracias.*"

Emilio leaped to his feet in silent applause. Someone else in the shadows at the back of the room left abruptly. Sandro had thought they were alone. *What is the punishment for impersonating a priest?*

After the Mass, as Emilio took the vestments, he said, "Where you come from they must say the Mass differently, *sí?*"

"Well, yes, yes, I suppose we do." Sandro, not wanting to be drawn into a discussion about which he knew nothing, suggested they be on their way.

They passed a middle-aged priest, who stopped them. "An intriguing sermon, Padre Sandro. Altogether fascinating. How long has it been since you took Holy Orders?"

"Three years. But now we shall hurry to the refectory, for I must continue my pilgrimage. God be with you."

§

Padre Emilio walked Sandro across town to the bridge over the River Bernesga. The pilgrims' route left León from this spot. Sandro pushed the bicycle while Puntillo rode behind in stately silence.

As they crossed a square a truck skidded to a halt and four Guardias jumped out. They quickly arrested three workers on the street and hauled them away.

As Sandro and Padre Emilio neared the river, the pair were greeted by a member of a gang of workers.

"*Hola.* We are miners from Asturias. Although I do not like priests, I don't mind asking them for directions." The man named a street and Padre Emilio gave him instructions.

"Why are you in León?" Sandro ventured.

"We have come to defend the Republic, to begin the *Revolución*. Four thousand others will soon follow. Have you not heard? There are rumours the fascists are about to attempt a coup. Once León is secured, we will go on to Madrid. But why do I tell this to a priest?" He looked at his cronies. "Because I have supreme confidence that the Revolution will succeed. *Nuestra Revolución.*" He saluted with a raised fist and the crowd did the same.

Padre Emilio shrugged, "I do not understand politics."

Sandro watched the miners retreat.

"I understand it all too well."

The long low bridge over the Bernesga stood next to the Palace of San Marcos, a sprawling Renaissance building, with a plateresque façade crammed with carved soldier heads, garlands of fruit, scallop shells, candelabras and plump stone cherubs.

"It was once a hostel for pilgrims," said Emilio. "Now it is in ruins. Like Spain, *sí?* I must return now. Bless you on the remainder of your journey. God go with you."

As Sandro walked toward the bridge, he saw several old men playing a game of bowls on the sand. The late-morning sun was scorching hot. Everything was white hot and aflame: the buildings, the trees, the old men. They played on a flat patch of pounded earth and sand next to the slow rolling river. Nine wooden cones, each about knee-high, stood equally spaced on the playing court. They were trying to knock down a smaller cone in the centre with an underhand toss of a wooden hemisphere, about the size of a small melon cut in half. It sailed in an arc through the air and landed among the cones but missed "killing" the small cone, which he heard one of the men refer to as the "spy". This had to be done without "waking up", that is, knocking over, the "soldiers" guarding the spy. It seemed as if the old men had been there for a thousand years and would be there still in a thousand more.

A small wiry fellow had just made his toss when a flash in the corner of Sandro's eye made him turn his head. He stared wide-eyed at a young man, a bystander, near the bridge railing. Like an image out of a medieval nightmare, he was enveloped in flames twice his height, staggering onto the bowls court! The young man stumbled then collapsed, facedown.

The players shouted, "*Qué?! Cuidado! Socorro! Socorro!*" and one tore off his black coat and tried to throw it over the young man, but was driven back by the intense heat. Sandro stood helplessly and watched in disbelief, his legs weak, his stomach churning. People screamed for a doctor, but Sandro knew it was too late. The brilliance of the fire hurt his eyes.

As the flames died to sputtering blue lancets, the crowd quieted as well. They stood in a circle, trying to fathom what had happened. The cones were scattered. The young man had fallen on top of the "spy" at the centre. Sandro turned to look at the faces around him. Suddenly nothing made sense.

Maybe this is it. Maybe this madness, this inexplicable locura, *marks the start of war.* Sandro stared at his shaking hands. He looked at the black outline on the ground. *It could be me.*

As if in a dream, Sandro climbed onto Libertad and pushed off across the bridge, gripping the handlebars hard to keep from shaking. He rode without thinking, trying to put the terrible image out of his head.

Ten minutes along the road, Sandro spotted a fruit-seller among the shops that lined the street near the outskirts of the city. Apples, pears and walnuts were displayed in baskets out front. As Sandro swung off the bicycle, Puntillo fluttered up onto the eaves.

"The road north to Cascantes? Do you know it?"

"*Sí, sí*." The man pointed directly across the way. "This one goes to Cascantes." He went about his tasks.

Sandro noticed another bicycle in the distance. As it drew near, he recognized the hulk of the inspector leaning over the handlebars. He kept his back to the street and took furtive glances over his shoulder. Gonzalo slowed at the turn to Cascantes. He stopped and gazed down the side road that led north, then wheeled the bike toward the fruit-seller's.

Sandro turned up his collar and prepared to flee, but before he could take a step Puntillo, with a piercing *grawk grawk*, swept down from the eaves and dived at the inspector. As before, he threw up his hands, leaped on his bicycle and sped down the road heading west. The crow followed, diving at the back of the policeman's head. The terrified Gonzalo ducked, waved his right hand above and behind him and pedaled harder still. The inspector, his *bicicleta* and Puntillo da Parrapunte were soon out of sight.

Sandro waited a while to see if the crow would return. When he did not, Sandro hopped on Libertad and took the road for Cascantes. *I suspect old Puntillo will harry that inspector all the way to Santiago.*

Sandro was deep in the countryside by mid-afternoon. He halted and crawled into a hedgerow near a river. Removing his priest's cassock and hiding it under the brush, he dressed in a shirt and pair of pants from his suitcase. He could easily be murdered in the north merely for being a priest.

He slept, ate, and wrote a letter to Teresa. With the first signs of approaching dusk, he took to the road, the snow-capped Picos de Europa mountains before him. He rode all night without incident.

Dear Teresa,

Perhaps I am mad, perhaps you live only in these letters and that fateful week we spent together was nothing but hallucination. For the first time, my confidence is waning. My strength flags and I begin to wonder if I can reach home. So many strange things have happened of late, I cannot begin to tell you.

You will be happy to hear I am no longer a priest. It would be dangerous for me to continue to pose as a cleric where I am heading now. The guerra *draws near. I suspect it may have already begun. I can see it in people's eyes. I can hear it in their voices, the tightness in their throats. They are afraid. We are all afraid.*

Sandro

§

Sandro pulled into the yard of an inn in the village of Cascantes. Sprigs of lavender grew along one wall where a turtledove stood against the morning sky. A cock was crowing, while a young woman, her hair in a long black braid, walked from the henhouse back to the inn, five brown eggs nestled in her apron.

"*Buenos días*," said Sandro.

"*Santo cielo!* You surprised me." She smiled, then looked shyly at her bare feet.

"Can I get something to eat here and a room for the night, perhaps several nights?"

"*Sí. Claro.* You are most welcome. Where have you come from?"

"From León. I was a *peregrino* on the Saint James Way, but now I am heading home, a village in the north, on the sea."

"I will take you to my mother and father. My name is Camino. Half the girls in our village are called Camino, named after the Virgin of the Road."

Three nights. Maybe four.

The rustic inn bustled with activity. Camino's parents greeted him as if he were their own child, home from his travels. *Five nights.*

"You are a welcome guest here," said Camino's portly mother, "free to stay as long as you wish."

"*Gracias. Muchas gracias,*" Sandro nodded and, for the first time in weeks, he began to relax.

§

The man leaned across the table and stared at Sandro. "You'll need a revolver. At some point in your journey you will thank me. Go ahead, take it." The *pistola*, grey and oily, lay on the table before them. A retired colonel from the Spanish foreign legion, Aurelio Sanchez was a regular at the inn. He had befriended Sandro and spoke to him of the greatness of an officer he had known in Morocco, General Francisco Franco y Bahamonde, "the only man who can save this country."

The colonel had silver hair, and was pale, thin, bitter. His mouth twisted when he spoke of the *comunistas* or the anarchists. But he directed the bulk of his anger at the Republic, which he believed to be a government of traitors. "They have allowed chaos to rule the country. Only the generals can set things straight now. You will see." He glared at Sandro. "Punishment must be meted out, *nuestra España* must have its vengeance. Soon you too will defend our country from those who would spit on its glorious past. You are young yet, but you will see."

The colonel was the only person Sandro had met in Cascantes who had any interest whatsoever in the outside world. The others at the inn tried to avoid the man entirely. Naively unaware of his reputation, Sandro, at first, had felt obliged to listen.

Now, on this, their third evening, the colonel had slowly lifted the revolver from beneath the table and placed it between them. "You will need it up north."

Camino moved among guests serving *fabada,* bread and wine.

Sandro stared at the revolver. *Perhaps the pistol will prove useful.* In a moment of weakness he picked it up. He glanced at Camino, who moved with a sensuous grace, unhurried, soft. He felt her warmth, even from a distance, watched as she bent over the earthenware water jar in the corner. She reminded him of Teresa. He slipped the *pistola* into his waistband, under his shirt.

§

Jagged peaks ahead and behind, dizzying precipices to the side, the Picos de Europa were both beautiful and perilous. He had seen no one for two days, save a couple of blackened coal miners heading back to their hovels. A few sheepfolds of lichen-covered stone dotted the landscape. His legs ached, he could feel his kneecaps rolling under the skin, his ankles and toes were sore. All around him was grey rock, nothing green, nothing alive. Although climbing the mountains in the heat was unbearable, it was too dangerous to ride at night because of the switchbacks and cliffs.

Sandro began to walk his bicycle up the steep road, but when he reached the crest he realized there was another beyond that and another still beyond that. His heart sank. *Rest. A bit of water. A small bite to eat.* Not far from where he stopped he could see a field of snow. It startled him. *Qué idiota! If I am caught up here at night, I will freeze!* He finished his water and apple and was on his way.

For a few hundred metres he was refreshed and then the pain returned, redoubled, to his legs. He pumped on, like a drunkard weaving up the hill. The hard leather seat of the bicycle had rubbed the insides of his thighs raw. He grimaced and pushed, stood then sat again. He grit his teeth, gripped the handlebars, ground the wheels around ...

He must have blacked out for when he snapped to the bicycle was rolling backwards down the mountain! Suddenly it struck a rock and Sandro fell twisting to the ground, knocking his head in the process.

Pain shot through his limbs. He stumbled to his feet, dizzy, and vomited. His left elbow felt broken or at least seriously bruised. His arm was studded with pebbles; blood ran between his fingers. He walked in circles, trying to shake off the pain. His left thigh was sore.

Libertad had suffered only a loose chain. He worked it back on and wiped the grease on his pants. He sat for several minutes, thinking of nothing. In an icy stream he washed his arm, soaked his face and filled his waterskin. *I must hurry.*

He pedaled through a cool mist — he was bicycling through the belly of a ghost. He could see no more than a few metres ahead.

Suddenly, the mist rose. Snowfields surrounded him. He stopped and removed the revolver from his bag. He felt its weight, smelled its oily odour. He took aim at the sun and fired. The retort echoed, tearing through the empty sky and deep valleys. He flung the revolver into the air and watched it tumble into the crags below.

Minutes later he was tearing down the mountain road, hoping his brakes would hold, as he zigzagged back and forth, short bursts of speed followed by a slight application of the brakes — *tchew, tchew* — for each slow, curling turn. He sped down and down and down, twisting and turning back into the world.

Where the road finally flattened out, he encountered another roadblock. He had nowhere to run or to hide, surrounded on both sides by fields.

"*Alto!*" said a sergeant, uselessly, for Sandro was already halted and waiting. A lieutenant approached.

"Name?" said the lieutenant.

"José Sender." A former schoolmate in Barcelona.

"Do you know this man?" The lieutenant handed a telegram to Sandro.

ADVISE ARREST CRIMINAL LEFTIST - STOP - NAMED
SANDRO RISCO CÁNOVAS - STOP - BICYCLING OVER
PICOS DE EUROPA - STOP - HAS PISTOLA - STOP -
DANGEROUS - STOP - COLONEL AURELIO SANCHEZ -
STOP

"No, I don't know this Cánovas."

"Where are you from?"

"Arcasella, on the coast."

"Yes, I know of this place. And what are you doing here?"

"I was a *peregrino* on the Saint James Way. Now I am going home."

"I see. Open your bag. Do you have any weapons? A *pistola,* perhaps?" Sandro shook his head.

"Search his person, Sergeant."

The guard patted Sandro's pockets and his waistband.

"*Nada.*"

The lieutenant opened the suitcase and began rooting through its contents. He pulled out the canvas bag of pigments and held it up. "What are these?"

"For painting ..."

At that moment a Guardia approached on a motorcycle, stopped hastily, let the motorcycle drop at his feet and ran up to the lieutenant. "The miners!" he shouted, waving his hands. "Come quickly! They are attacking the armoury!"

The lieutenant dropped the bag and sprinted for his truck, followed by a half-dozen other men.

The sergeant paused and looked back. "What about him? Shouldn't I shoot him?"

"Leave him. Hurry!"

Sandro stood frozen by the side of the road for several minutes before he picked up the canvas bag and repacked his suitcase, strapping it onto Libertad. He took a side road until he reached a cluster of hazel trees and fell into an exhausted sleep.

The next day he continued through several villages and finally arrived in Oviedo by nightfall. *Now it begins. All has changed and the darkness comes. What awaits me on the other side?*

§

Sandro pedaled warily into Oviedo. The city was in chaos: people ran across plazas, carts tipped over on every street, burning automobiles littered the streets. No one could tell him if the roads to Gijón and Arcasella were still open.

"Come join us, comrade," a tall, bearded labourer shouted as he raced down the street and around a corner.

Heavy gunfire sounded near the armoury. Each street he turned down had more fires than the last, more men leaning out of doorways and firing into the night. At the end of one street half a dozen miners knelt behind a pair of dead horses and fired at imaginary movements.

Someone in a doorway reached out and pulled him in. "Get out of there! You'll be shot!" A woman stood holding a baby in her arms. "*Venga!*" she said, motioning for Sandro to follow her into the cellar.

A single oil lamp lit the musty, windowless room. A little boy of about three stared wide-eyed from behind a blanket in the corner, its edge stained white where he had been sucking it. The woman sat at a table and began to nurse the baby. She had a strong, heavy face and dark eyes.

"I have been watching for my husband from that doorway for two hours. He has still not returned. Put your *bicicleta* over by the wall. We are not thieves. It will be safe."

"I was a student in Barcelona, but I am trying to get home, to Arcasella, by the sea."

"That will be difficult. There is much fighting now, all around Oviedo. My husband tells me many of the generals have turned against the Republic. Garrisons have revolted. In Oviedo they are for the fascists. Meanwhile, the Reds and the anarchists are murdering priests and nuns, burning churches. The anarchists or the *comunistas*, no one is sure, have attacked the armoury, but have not taken it yet. They say soldiers siding with the coup executed forty men outside Oviedo this morning, but no one knows what to believe."

Sandro sat at the table, trying to decide what to do.

"Have you eaten? In the kitchen upstairs I have some soup. It will be cold now, but you are welcome to it."

They went up the stairs and entered the kitchen. Window glass lay scattered on the floor. She tilted the pot to pour a bowl of bean soup and then they returned downstairs where she poured him a cup of wine from a jug on the table. After eating, Sandro stretched out on the blanket next to the little boy.

Half an hour later, the woman shook him gently by the shoulder. "It is quiet now. Perhaps you could escape into the countryside before it starts up again."

Sandro stared sleepily into her large eyes. "Has your husband returned?"

She drew a shawl around her shoulders and looked away.

§

From behind a knobby apple tree on a high hillside, Sandro watched what was unfolding below. A long column of men marched along the road, a half dozen of them with rifles pointed at twenty prisoners roped together in a line. None of the guards wore uniforms. The column stopped in an orchard on the far side of the road. The prisoners were ordered to kneel among the apple trees. Two of the guards appeared drunk and were dressed in clerical garb — a bishop's hat and cassock. They stumbled about, laughing and swigging from a wine bottle. Casually they let off shots, a sound like rocks splitting open. Dark red stains appeared on the backs of the prisoners' shirts. They lay twisted and ignored by the guards, who walked calmly back to the road. One smashed the empty bottle against a boulder.

The birds chirped as if nothing had happened.

When he was sure they had gone, Sandro approached the bodies. A thin boy of about fourteen lay on his back, a weak moan rising from his chest. His eyes, fixed on the sky, were moist and empty.

Sandro lifted him. "I will take you to the next village." The boy groaned and bit his lip as Sandro sat him on the suitcase so he could lean against Sandro as he pedaled.

The streets of the village were deserted, except for a lone mongrel that barked as they passed. At the end of the plaza stood an ancient stone church. Sandro hurried up the steps, peeked in the doors — a mass was in progress. He went back to get the boy, but it was too late. He lay on the bike, a trickle of red spittle dripping into the spokes. *Maldita sea*! Sandro hissed. He lifted the boy in his arms, climbed the stairs and entered the church. All eyes turned to him, and to the body draped in his arms, head tilted backwards, one shoe missing. He walked down the aisle, climbed two steps and deposited the boy on the altar.

Sandro waited.

"He is not from our village," said the priest, as the worshippers filed to the front to view the body.

§

In the next two days Sandro passed a number of roadblocks, most of them set up by supporters of the Republic. Though some of the men looked like regular soldiers, others were simply nervous peasants with rifles, or armed bands of boyish thugs.

Once, he was recognized by a soldier who said he knew Sandro's father; he was free to pass. At another roadblock, an old Guardia Civil looked him in the eye and said, "You are brown from the sun. A face worthy of trust or I am no judge of character. You look like my brother's son in Gijón, a young fellow about your age. Hurry home to see your *madre* and then come back and join us in our fight." He tossed Sandro an apple as he left.

§

In the next village, Sandro descended a street narrowed by two stone walls as it emptied into the town plaza. There he passed a monastery, one of its oversize doors ajar and hanging off its hinge. The building's interior was a yawning black hole that sucked in the hard light of day.

Figures were propped up against the wall near the door, two were slumped over on the steps, three were seated at odd angles in a shady corner. He halted by a fountain, his heart pounding. He looked about him in horror. They were half-rotted corpses, bones visible at the ends of coat sleeves, eye sockets empty, skin the colour of leather. Two bodies floated in the red water of the fountain. Open coffins were strewn about the plaza. He grabbed a handkerchief to cover his nose and mouth against the stench. Someone had come, killed the priests and emptied the coffins from the monastery crypt, setting up the corpses in a morbid tableau.

In a butcher shop nearby he saw four corpses hung on meat hooks, faces contorted, their arms tied behind them. A hand-scratched sign had been attached to one of them: HOY MATADO, "freshly killed." Sandro backed out to the buzzing of flies.

How is such a thing possible? For the first time, he wondered what he would find in his own village. *Will anyone be there? Will everyone have fled? To the mountains? The sea?* He was too stunned, too sickened, too angry to weep.

§

The next day, Sandro rounded a bend atop a cliff and saw the sea in the distance, waves of white foam breaking on the beach. He took a deep breath of salt air. He could see Arcasella down the coast, its two headlands jutting into the ocean, a swath of beach between them. From where he stood, he could take in the whole village: the two promontories, the white arc of sand, the river, the bridge, the grey and brown stone buildings, the church and its bell tower.

An hour later, just before the bridge into Arcasella, he took a road that cut right and climbed a hill. There stood his family *casa* — part farmhouse, part fisherman's hut.

His mother's rude garden appeared overgrown and disheveled. The house was surrounded by a couple of small sheds and a tiny barn, enough to hold a few goats and a donkey. He cycled to the nearest shed, pulled open the door and left Libertad in the dim light. He did not want any passersby to see the bicycle and question his family. Through the back door he slipped into the house.

She turned heavily from where she stood over a bowl on a counter and stared at him as if he were a ghost. She tilted her head, one hand held gently near her throat. "Sandro?"

"I have come home."

His mother looked out the window. "Did anyone see you?"

He shook his head.

She held out her arms, kissed him all over the face and they hugged for a long time. She ran her hand through his thick black hair and whispered his name over and over.

"Where is Papa?" he asked.

"At sea. He returns this evening. Lord God of Angels, I can't believe you are safe." She blessed herself.

"And Pedro? Where is my brother?"

She shook her head and held back tears.

"What is it, Mama?"

"They came and took him two weeks ago. The Cruzado brothers. They said he must fight with the Falangists. I could do nothing. Your papa was away." Her eyes went dark with pain.

Sandro collapsed in a chair. "If only I had come sooner."

"No." She waved her finger, adamant. "No. I would have lost two sons. You could not have stopped them. They had rifles. They threatened to shoot me if Pedro refused to go with them."

Sandro pounded the wooden table with both fists.

"They mustn't know you have returned or they will come for you, too. You must hide." She glanced out the window. "What will we do?"

"I have a plan."

"You must not be seen here. Come to the barn."

§

What is that sound? I believe it is the wind whistling in my ears, as I step from a boat toward dry land and ... Teresa awakened from the dream to the shrill wail of sirens. It was 5:00 a.m. Darkness had begun to fade. July 19. Jorge snored on his makeshift bed on the floor. He had recovered sufficiently for Teresa to reclaim her own bed, but still he stayed on, knowing he could be arrested immediately if recognized on the street. She didn't mind — it helped relieve her loneliness. She did not speak of it to him, but she lived a life cut off from others: few knew that she was a member of POUM. She sat up. *The sirens. It has begun.*

Teresa went to the window. A few people had already run out from their apartments into the street. Each window on her block framed a figure standing at it, looking out on the new and terrible world.

In minutes she was on the street herself. She stopped a labourer who was hurrying past.

"Yes, it has begun. The military is rising against the Republic! People are needed at the docks. Follow me!"

In a short while a crowd of several hundred workers had streamed into the dock area. In the far distance they saw three batteries of artillery advancing on them, pushed by soldiers. One worker, wearing a red bandana, shouted amidst the confusion: "We must stop them!"

Several others ran to a warehouse and broke open the doors. The warehouse was filled with huge bales of paper that could be used as barricades. Two workers with old rifles took up position behind them and begin firing at the artillery. Teresa leaned against a bale. *Paper. Soon to be posters, banners and manifestos, newspapers and cheap magazines. A barricade of paper.*

She felt a tap on her shoulder. "Follow me." It was her cell leader, José. They ran from the barricade, as more workers arrived with guns and began handing them out to people who needed to be shown how to use them.

In a nearby alley, José stopped. "What are you doing here? I don't want you to be seen, I told you."

"What has happened?"

"The military in many parts of the country has risen against us. Here the Guardia Civil is still loyal to the Republic. Our luck holds, for the moment. The Guardia will always side with the likeliest winner. We could lose them tomorrow, next week or next month. And the air force may not be far behind. Now go. Your work is too important for you to be lost now. I will be in contact shortly."

§

Not five minutes after Teresa had returned to her apartment, there came a knock at the door. Jorge slipped into a large broom closet in a corner of the kitchen while Teresa went to the door and opened it slowly.

A tall blond man stood in the hall and nodded. "Teresa Maza? I am Adam Weatherhead, a friend of Sandro's."

She looked at him blankly.

"May I come in?"

"How do I know you are a friend of Sandro's?"

"I met him on the road. He was cycling to Arcasella. I'm afraid you'll just have to trust me."

She let him in. Adam entered the apartment and looked about.

"You have some news from Sandro?" Teresa motioned Adam to a seat in the kitchen. She stood with her hands gripping the back of a chair, longing to hear, afraid to hear.

"Yes, I left him about three weeks ago. We spent some time together — hiding, in a tree. When we split up, he gave me this to deliver to you." Adam pulled a bundle of letters from his inside coat pocket and handed it to Teresa. He explained that Sandro was likely somewhere north of León, near his family home. "He's probably in the Picos de Europa mountains by now."

Teresa looked at the letters and put them in a cupboard — she would devour them later.

"I'm also looking for a friend of Sandro's named Jorge Sentis. Do you know where I might find him?"

Teresa smiled. "Jorge," she called, "it's safe."

Jorge emerged from the broom closet. He limped over to Adam. "You are a friend of Sandro's? Then you are also a friend of mine." The two men shook hands.

For the next three hours, and throughout a meal of salted cod stew, the three spoke about Sandro. Adam told them in detail about their time in the tree and everything he could remember about Sandro's journey to that point. At last, he thanked them and asked how he might find POUM headquarters.

"They'll need me," he said.

§

Late that night, after Jorge had fallen asleep, Teresa rose from bed and went to the cupboard. She sat at the kitchen table and read the letters slowly, savouring each word. When she had finished, she took them to the window and held them over a candle flame, as she had with her own letters. A ribbon of smoke wafted up to the stars, drifting westward.

§

In Barcelona the military coup was defeated in battles at the Placa de Catalunya and Sant Pau Gate. Coup leaders were dragged away and executed. Elsewhere in Spain, however, the military uprising was a success and Franco flew in from North Africa with his battle-hardened, brutal Moorish troops to claim control. Franco's supporters took the cities of Pamplona, Seville, Vigo, Segovia, Burgos and many others across Spain.

Within weeks, the front was established and men could be seen on the streets of Barcelona in the uniforms of a ragtag army: corduroy knee breeches, puttees or corduroy gaiters, leather leggings, high boots, zippered jackets of leather or wool, red or red-and-black handkerchiefs about their throats. They wore their party badges — CNT, FAI, UGT, POUM, PSUC — on the fronts of their caps.

On every street corner, people spoke excitedly about the war, about the Revolution, about what would happen. The air was electric and chaotic.

Teresa said to Jorge, "It's happening just as I thought it would — too many opinions, too many political stripes. It will kill us. Our country is being invaded by Moors, the Moors we threw out hundreds of years ago!"

In the following days, the streets of Barcelona were taken up with the heady celebrations of revolution. Industries were collectivized. Workers took power. Every building was draped in red flags or flags of red and black. The hammer and sickle, party acronyms or posters exhorting victory covered walls everywhere. Workers were recognized by their dungarees or blue overalls and hemp sandals. Everyone said "*salud*" instead of "*buenos días*."

"It's idiotic," Teresa shook her head. "Today I saw a pile of furniture on the Ramblas. It had been dragged out of a wealthy family's apartment. There was a grand piano with an axe embedded in it. A man can be taken away and shot for saying '*buenos días*.' Assassination squads are murdering nuns and priests, shooting them against cemetery walls. Churches are being gutted and burned. It sickens me. It will come back to haunt us."

Jorge bowed his head, and went back to reading the CNT newspaper. She was beginning to think the Revolution for Jorge was constructed of words and words alone.

Along the Ramblas loudspeakers bellowed revolutionary songs as people waited in long queues for a bit of coal or sugar. Truckloads and trainloads of volunteers left for the front every day, shouting, "*No pasarán!* They shall not pass!"

Late one Sunday night, Adam left, too. He would spend a full week at the front before he was even issued a gun.

At Teresa's café, the clientele changed. There were no more soldiers, only a few militia, some assault guards who had helped crush the uprising. The communists of PSUC claimed three tables at the rear and would appear each night to argue. They were Stalinists. One night they rose to toast their Georgian hero. Teresa, as always, served beer and brandy and wine and listened, her face blank.

A Russian at the table claimed, "Nin and his POUM colleagues, they are nothing but Trotskyites."

A hard-looking woman spoke up: "He even looks like Trotsky, that Andres Nin, with his little round glasses and intellectual air."

Teresa held her tongue and listened.

The Cave at Arcasella

The scratch of a wooden match woke Sandro from a dreamless sleep. From his makeshift bed in the hay he could see his father sitting before him on a stool, lighting his pipe, the door of the small barn half open. The pipe was lost in his fist, the knuckles under shiny stretched skin.

His father puffed, puffed again, looked in the bowl of the short pipe, repacked the tobacco with a bent finger, stuffed the pipe into his mouth, slid open the box of matches, struck a match and re-lit the pipe. He flicked the dead match out the door. His full white moustache was stained brown at the tips.

"It has been too long, Sandro, too long," he said.

"Papa."

"You slept well?"

Sandro nodded. He watched his father's languid but methodical motions. A goat bleated in the distance. "How's the fishing?"

His father turned his hand, palm up, palm down.

Sandro pulled bits of straw from his hair, wondering how his father could have aged so much in one year.

"Mama says you have decided to hide. *Aquí?*"

"No, not here. It's too dangerous."

"Where then?"

"I don't know."

"Sandro." Agustín removed the pipe. "Do not lie to me."

"Papa, it would be dangerous to tell you. If the soldiers come ..."

He nodded. "*Sí.* I understand. Better we do not know." He paused and fussed with the pipe again. "It will be hard. How will you live?"

"I will come to the house at night to get food and whatever else I need. Do not leave anything out for me — no messages. I must remain invisible."

"Your mama thinks you will not need to hide for long. I fear she is wrong. When will you go?"

"*Esta noche.*"

"Too bad you cannot hide at sea. I could visit you there."

Sandro shrugged. "The sea is no place to hide."

Agustín nodded. "You are right. Only the dead hide there." He paused, then said, "The Cruzado brothers took your brother to fight for the Falange — those gutless *cabrones.*"

"Mama told me."

"I was at sea, I could do nothing." He spat.

"They would have killed you."

Agustín puffed. "The next day the Reds came for him. I told them, 'the Falange already took him'."

"Did they believe you?"

"One look at your mama's face told the truth."

"Papa, if the Falange come and ask about me, tell them the communists dragged me off. I was stopped at many roadblocks on the way here, so someone might know I have returned. If the Reds come, tell them the Falange have taken me."

§

It took Sandro half a day, following his mother's directions, to climb the mountain path that twisted through the forest and over corrugated streams to the high meadow. As he walked he thought about Pedro. Sandro remembered late one winter, when the boys were half grown and food was so scarce that people had started to eat their goats, cows and donkeys. The fishing was terrible. Old people were consulted for their knowledge of edible winter plants. Sandro and his brother walked in on their mother in tears. Agustín had just returned from a two-day fishing trip with a single medium-size hake. They sat down to dinner that night and divided two small potatoes, the shining hake and one wrinkled apple among the four of them. But Agustín pretended they were about to feast. He put a small round stone on everyone's plate and said this was to be sucked between courses, because that is what the Spanish kings and queens did. He convinced everyone. Pedro laughed so hard his stomach tightened and he was less aware of his hunger. Even Mercedes smiled shyly.

Sandro came to a field and spied a stone hut, more like a sheepfold than a house, and walked through the knee-high grass toward it.

The *divina* stood at the door, waiting for him.

"You are Balma, the *divina*?"

"You know I am she."

Sandro nodded. "*Mi madre*, Mercedes, has sent me."

"A good woman. She fares well?"

"No. It would be a lie to say she is well. These are ... difficult times."

The *divina,* squinting in the light, was tall, thin, dressed in an old threadbare shift. Her fingers were exceedingly long, with knucklebones the size of walnuts. She squinted into the light and didn't look at Sandro when she spoke, but focused her gaze on the distant mountains somewhere beyond his left shoulder.

"You have lost a cow? I can find it for you." This was normally her role.

"No."

"A goat?"

"No."

"A sheep, then? *Un caballo?* Maybe a pig. You have lost a pig? How odd to lose a pig. They usually do not get lost. Well, come in, sit down, get out of the sun and I will tell you where your pig has gone."

"I have not lost a pig. I've lost a brother. *Mi hermano*, Pedro."

Balma frowned. "Come in, young Sandro. It is Sandro? Yes, I remember, the one with the Italian name. Come in."

She wasn't as old as she looked, but years of lonely isolation in the mountains had left her worn and grey.

Sandro sat down across from her. Resting on the table was a large crucifix, the figure of Christ pale and wasted. She picked it up and waved it in the air a few times. A rooster, likely thinking she was tossing grain, fluttered onto the table. She batted it across the room with the crucifix and gave it an evil look. "*Cállate!*" Turning to Sandro, she sighed. "My dead husband."

"I see."

"I must not speak of it. The church frowns on such things."

Sandro nodded. A silence settled on the room. Through the gloom he saw the house was furnished with a bed, a chest and a stone shelf weighed down with several crocks and cloth bags.

"I have brought some apples." Sandro placed the bag on the table.

As Balma removed the bag, not bothering to look inside, but placing it at her feet, she said, "I do not believe in witches. Hardly anyone ever gets possessed any more. What will be done with all the useless Jesuits?"

She turned around in her chair, then spun back. "But some things are indisputable. I have seen them myself. In here." She pointed to her left temple.

"Do you know where my brother Pedro is?"

She paused a moment and closed her eyes, her left index finger still at her temple, her eyelids heavily veined. Slowly she removed her finger. "I see him. He is hiding."

"He is alive? Where is he hiding?"

"He hides in the mountains," she said matter-of-factly.

She opened her eyes. "I also see you hiding. In a cave. For a long time. Alone. Like me. Alone for many seasons. The priest said to read the Gospels to cure madness. He had balls the size of raisins. Not like my old husband. A man who could have mated with mares."

Sandro wasn't listening to her, but gazed at the floor, then out the window.

The *divina* put her right index finger over her lips. "I am a crazy old woman, but I am sure. Pedro is with bad men. *No entiendo.*"

"I must ask you something very important. Do you think I should leave the village? I have seen terrible things, things I did not think possible. And now Pedro has been taken. Perhaps I should take my mother and father and get away — to sea, or perhaps to the mountains?"

"I see no harm coming to them. Have good Mercedes make you a large corn cake to take with you."

She closed her eyes again, "I see it. *La cueva*. Many lost animals are there; the animals have turned to stone." She opened her eyes. "You must go alone."

Sandro nodded.

"After three days he rose from the dead. Not Pedro. You." She chuckled.

The rooster pecked in the dust under the table. Balma reached down and took the bird into her lap, smoothing its feathers.

§

A pool of swampy water fronted the cave entrance and thick vines trailed down over the hole, covering it completely. Sandro was only able to see inside when an arm's length away.

He entered, lit the candle and checked the wooden boxes stacked where he had left them the summer before, just inside the cave entrance. They appeared odd, piled as if on a train platform awaiting shipment, slatted wooden crates of pine, solid and mysterious.

When he was young he had told no one about the cave, except his brother Pedro, and he was sure that no one else in the village knew about it. He went there only when he wanted privacy and when his absence would not invite questions. Both his parents and his brother had grown used to his need for solitude.

Over time he had explored the cave thoroughly, following the twisting stone passages deeper and deeper into the earth, searching the many side channels by candlelight. Eventually he found the great hall. For hours he sat listening to the silence, going deeper and deeper into it.

Sandro looked over the boxes again. The fact that they had remained untouched since the previous summer assured him the cave remained a secret. It would take many hours to carry the crates along the twisting path to the last chamber.

He opened the flour sack containing food, clothes and blankets, his sketchbook, the pigments, a crowbar and other tools he'd brought from his parent's home. At the last moment he had remembered to throw in a dozen boxes of matches and a roll of wick.

He opened the first box with the crowbar: cans of kerosene and a simple oil lantern. He lit the lamp and placed it on top of the box then hoisted the wooden crate to waist level, taking care not to extinguish the lamp as he made his way through the cave.

Shadows danced around him. *Already the silence penetrates me to the core.* On reaching the hall, he set the box down, lifted the oil lamp by its handle, turned and walked back for the next crate.

§

The next morning Sandro asked his father to post a letter. Although the post office was still open, it was hard to say how the mail would travel during wartime. That done, he pushed Libertad to an abandoned barn at the edge of a nearby field. He wheeled the bike to the far corner, burying it in piles of old hay.

That night, after a dinner punctuated by long silences, Sandro said farewell to his mother and father and headed into the darkness.

Dear Teresa,

I believe this will be my last letter for many months. I do not know if mail is getting through, but I pray this reaches you and that you have not forgotten me or, worse, think that I have forgotten you. Did the letters I sent with my friend Adam ever reach you?

I will tell you where I am, at long last. I am in hiding, but when the war finishes (soon, I hope), I will return to the home of my parents, in a fishing village on the Cantabrian Sea called Arcasella. I believe you would like it there.

My brother Pedro has been taken to fight with the Falange. I hope he is safe and not made to suffer. He is a gentle soul and I fear he would perish quickly if he were forced to fight.

I have traveled by bicycle across the north of Spain following the old pilgrim way toward Santiago de Compostela. After I left the Camino Santiago I turned north at León and came over the Picos de Europa mountains to my village.

The journey over the mountains was difficult, but nothing compared to the frightful scenes I witnessed in the villages and fields along the road after Oviedo; the war has started in earnest.

Each day the sun comes up and the sea tides shift and the waves break along the arc of beach at the foot of our village. This will continue even after the war has finished, no matter who has won.

Nothing attained too easily is worth having. I sense you understand that. I see now that you are truly my only route to freedom. Goodbye. Remember me.

In love and sorrow,
Sandro

Mark Frutkin

§

I am in the cave at the bottom of the world. Dark ventricles, black galleries, creases and cavities twist deeper and deeper into the heart. The slow lightning of time, flashing not down from the sky but up out of earth. The earth's slow light, rising.

Sandro knew he would have only two enemies in the cave — loneliness and boredom. Both had the same cure.

The silence and the dark were absolute. *What does one do at the end of a pilgrimage, at the end of a long road? You come in from the scorching sun and rest. You agree to set freedom aside and be bound by the confines of a sacred space. You praise God, and if you have no God you praise Creation itself. You contemplate the world ... from within.*

Sandro groped for matches and lit the oil lamp. Flickers of light danced in a frieze on the bare stone walls. He snatched up the sketchbook and a piece of artist's charcoal. Again he had dreamed of the bull in a morning field. Although it seemed to float, he could feel its heaviness, the weight that held it to the earth.

He had dreamed of other beasts before, bison and mammoths, a herd of horses, a phalanx of sleek-horned ibexes, but most often he dreamed of the bull. He drew a single line on the page, beginning at the back of the neck and moving left to right to depict its hump. Again, a single line to show the short raised whip of tail, around and down a back leg, then curving up to the belly. Two short lines for the front legs. Another for the chest and throat. A rough squarish circle for the head and snout. A couple of short lines at the back of the neck and about the mouth. Two shallowly curved horns and the arc of an eye. Exactly as he had done, long ago, on a hillside near Linares.

Sandro had brought no wristwatch, no clock, no calendar. With alarming speed he had lost track of time. He slept when he felt tired, ate when hungry, worked constantly.

Occasionally he would explore the cave — its nooks and hollows, its side channels and tributaries. At night he would walk down to the cave mouth with a bucket and collect drinking water from a nearby stream or gather a handful of sticks for firewood. Sometimes he worked his way through the forest to the edge of the village and the house of his parents. Eyes and ears alert to the faintest sound, he would scan the table for a letter from Teresa. Swallowing his disappointment, he would toss vegetables and fruit, bags of rice and flour into a sack and scurry back.

Sitting on the cave's earthen floor, he looked at his hands. *Am I invisible? Is the world entirely lost to me now? Who am I?* From the deep recesses of darkness, there came no reply.

§

In this dark zone, each drop of water falling in black pools rings inside me. I hear a leaf drift, crumpling, in the distant wood. I open my eyes, light the lamp and the world shrinks to a space the size of my skull.

Sandro awakened and believed his eyes were open. He blinked. Like a cave-dwelling crab, his hand scrabbled around on the ground next to him for the matches. With a lit match clipped between thumb and index finger, its nervous flame twitching, he leaned toward the lamp. The flame quivered like a tiny figure of a man, a man draped in fire who swirled, arms raised to the heavens, dancing in light.

Sandro recalled the man in León who caught fire by the river.

Now, he is both outside and inside the man, watching him and yet feeling what he felt: the sun draws closer and closer and he longs for the first touch of its brilliance, longs to burn inside it, to be consumed, to have its fire purify him.

Now, dressed in a bison skin, its weight oppressive, its smell thick and meaty, he feels bound in its heat, his head inside its huge empty skull. He breathes its breath, sees through its eyes, tastes the bitterness of its saliva.

He lay back on the blanket and gazed at the ceiling. "It is time to begin," he said aloud. They are the first words — his own — he has heard spoken aloud in three weeks and they startle him.

§

On the far side of blackness I perceive an inconceivable brilliance. I go silent as a beast and set to work by the light of my flickering lamp.

Sandro inspected the pigments, setting them out in a line before him: limonite for yellow brown; red, yellow and brown ochre; manganese dioxide for black; white kaolin; hematite. No blue, nothing of blue, for that was the colour of sky and would not enter here. He took a small tough branch from the pile next to his firewood and, with his knife, frayed a brushlike tip. He did the same with several other types of green wood. Shaking a touch of hematite powder onto a flat stone, he dipped one of the stick-brushes in his wooden water bucket, then swirled the stick in the powder and worked up a blood-red paste. He stood in the middle of the cave and turned in a circle.

Where to begin? How to begin? A circle, it has no beginning, no end. But one must start somewhere. And which way will it move?

Which animal came first? Which herd appeared first out of stone? They would appear as in a dream, with all the spontaneity and chaotic energy of hallucination. The animals would not be created of ground pigments and powders, not dust of kaolin and limonite, not stone, but of the flesh and breath and light that ignited their brains, their hearts, their bodies, their skin, their swirling candescent blood.

They would appear upside down, sideways, floating, overlapped, partially drawn, fragmented. He knew the only way he could let go was to immerse himself in the work, to lose himself in that world, to burst into flames — he felt himself falling, his head and hands and eyes ablaze.

A narrow crevice in the wall attracted him. He went to it, his arm and the stick-brush with its dollop of blood-red pigment bulbed at the tip extended toward the wall until the cleft in the stone bled into life.

§

I have walked corridors, felt damp walls, learned the turns and twists of this cave like the lines of my own palm. I hear the cave breathe before I fall asleep. I live inside a beast, lost in the dreams of a beast that burns, that turns colour, that fluoresces and fades over time. I go deeper, where the emptiness comes alive, where ibexes appear, stamping their hooves, where a bison chuffs, rumbles across the plain. I feel the earth shake, his shoulders ripple.

Once he had begun it poured from him with the turbulence of an underground river veined with skeins of crimson, vermilion, verdigris and maroon, soot black, chalk white, grey, orange, sulphur yellow, chestnut, umber. Deep colours. The colours of earth and bone and fire and ash. The colour of dried blood, lit by a deep internal sun. One beast bled into another, the animals alive and ranging in vibrant, overlapping, riotous herds around the cave walls, as if pouring from the original cleft. Random. Timeless.

He felt possessed, mad. He was no longer Sandro, but a man who had dreamed the primeval memories of beasts. Ecstatic, he slept and ate little, seldom left the cave. He had no idea if he had been painting for weeks, months or years. It was all that existed.

When he did leave the cave, he took his wooden bucket, went out into the fresh night and drank greedily from a stream. Like an animal he would defecate and urinate in the woods, and then he would return after finding a few dry sticks for his fire or small green stems for his brushes.

He stopped going to his parents' house and began eating food he found in the forest or nearby fields: tough, tart apples from wizened trees, chestnuts, hazelnuts, or wild mushrooms. Occasionally he would collect edible seaweed from the beach and make it into soup with wild greens.

The voice and face of Teresa still came to him, but less and less often. It was almost too painful to think of her, for he was alone now, utterly.

He even stopped longing for the night he would greet his father again, straight and stiff in his chair.

Have you been sitting up all night, Father?

Yes, my son. For many nights. We thought you had disappeared. The war is over, Sandro, over.

But it hadn't happened and Sandro seldom went to the house any more. The thought of seeing someone, anyone, filled him with dread.

§

Out of the cave mouth of brilliant, spinning blackness the beasts came pouring — horse head, hump of bison, horn of ibex. Like us, they breathe, breathe life and break into air and dissolve with time into the air from whence they came.

As he surfaced from sleep, a line from a sacred text spoke out of the bottomless dark: "It is precisely because He does not exist that God can so utterly love the world." Where did I read it? Long ago? In my previous life? Teresa of Ávila? Saint John of the Cross? Some unknown ecstatic or anchorite of the early church, a desert hermit, half pagan?

He opened his eyes and stared into blackness. Suddenly he was aware of the overwhelming power of the void inside and out. He felt only terror.

A roaring rushed in on him — a strange bestial wailing, cries, grunts, a language he had never heard before. The sound echoed off the walls in waves, as if the stone, the Earth itself and its deep memories were venting in tongues.

He fumbled for matches, lit the lamp. The cave appeared a terrifying and haunted place, filled with the unsettled presence of the dead. He was overpowered by a sense of claustrophobia, as if he were about to be buried alive.

He dressed and headed for the mouth of the cave, stepping around a gour, a shallow pool of water he had passed many times before. It was bubbling. When he reached the cave mouth, he leaned into the cool moist air, redolent with the scent of pine. He could see stars between branches. He blew out the lamp and walked into the forest.

Moments later he was climbing a towering chestnut tree, up through thick scaly branches, toward the night sky. The stars drew closer as he rose. The eastern sky before him turned slowly pink and yellow, the first soft light spreading westward. When the sun crested the horizon, like a boat appearing on the sea, it coated the surrounding clouds and hills in gold leaf.

He watched the world ignite. *To live is to burn.*

§

For a full week he was haunted by further attacks, by the cries of animals and the sound of stampeding. Each time he awoke, the infernal babble returned and he hurried to the cave mouth. *I must be going mad.* He had no desire to work. Finally, on awaking again to the chaos of whispers and cries, he picked up his brush and began to work. As he concentrated, the voices ebbed, quieted and dissolved. A hump-backed bison came to life before him.

§

A mythology of bones and flesh, breath and spark. The hoof sunk in the mud, horns spearing the air. The skin, brown and spotted, grunts heavily and lumbers to its feet. A hexagram of bones just visible under the thick leathery skin. A mythology of food and fertility and dreams and death. A mythology of light and dark. A mythology of struggle and birth and time. A mythology of the long silence, disturbed only by the murmur of the wind, the trembling of the sea, the faint purl of the bison's blood.

Sandro hesitated, turned from the wall to gaze into the darkness, holding a frayed twig in his hand, motionless, the black pigment at its tip shining. Am I dreaming again, or have I risen in the middle of the dream to paint?

He stared at a blank stone wall, but something was missing, both on the wall and inside himself. He longed for a bull to appear, to come alive before him, but he couldn't will it to life no matter how he tried. It was there, he knew it, yet it wouldn't rise to the surface.

Five arrows appeared on the wall, pointing left to right. They were simple, primitive, slightly arced with pointed ends. He placed his hand on the wall next to them. When he lifted it there appeared a footprint of a bull, its split hoof in sooty black pigment. He felt its weight.

He stared into the stone as if it were a mirror. A bull's head appeared, its eyes precise black jewels. The bull leaned forward, ready to charge, pure animal energy, a contained explosion of flesh barely restrained by skin. He felt its hot breath surging from its nostrils, the thick musculature of its neck, the solid sharpness of its horns.

A moment later the bull sat back on its haunches, as if tamed, its tail a thick whip shredded at the end, not unlike Sandro's brush. The bull rested, gazing at the ground. Then it leaped through the air, peaceful, light, sailing across the wall.

It dissolved into a mist of dots, random flicks of pigment. Sandro closed his eyes. When he opened them again, there was an empty circle on the wall before him. The eye of the bull.

He was in no hurry to finish. He let each stroke emerge from the stone, as if it already existed, as if his hand drew the image up out of the rock.

He was awake. He had no idea when the dream ended.

§

Let the world in the depths of its darkness burst into flames. Let light roar into the world, reducing it to ash and delivering it again whole, shining, radiant, empty.

Sandro stared up into the darkness, three thick blankets on top of him, the hard earth beneath. Out of nowhere her scent came to him — that smell he had almost forgotten: dusky rose, faint honeysuckle, the earth renewed after a summer rain. He saw her face, almost reached out and touched her. He fumbled for a match. By the time the light flashed, carving up the shadows, she had disappeared entirely.

§

Teresa stood staring into a dull mirror. Her face, once soft and sensuous, was now carved by hunger. No real bread for months. Little meat or fish. She dragged a brush through her hair. *Fools, what utter fools they all are.*

It was a spring without joy. She turned from the mirror as Jorge entered and slumped at the table.

"Day three, and I still cannot find a gun." Jorge's face was drawn. He had slept little for three nights, going out late each evening. "The PSUC Reds executed nine libertarians today. Nine! Young men gunned down! It's madness ..."

The Stalinists wanted to win the war then go on with the Revolution. The POUM communists and anarchists wanted the Revolution first.

Teresa sighed. "This is insane — a civil war within a civil war. And the workers don't know what they want — other than bread."

"They are saying the Soviet secret police are picking up POUM members and anarchists. Then they blame POUM for starting it." Jorge looked at Teresa. "I will take you away."

She didn't ask where.

§

After four days of confused fighting that killed five hundred people, the Republican government sent in assault guards from the city of Valencia to end it. The quiet in the month that followed was ominous.

Five weeks later, Teresa stood in a doorway across the street from her cell leader's apartment building. She had come in the middle of the night to warn him. At the café earlier that evening the Soviet agents, whose presence had increased considerably in the past few months, and the Catalan Stalinists, made little effort to hide what was about to unfold. A witch-hunt loomed. The POUM and anarchist leaders would be arrested. She had left the café as early as she could without raising suspicion.

She leaned from the doorway and looked across the street. A car was idling outside her cell leader's apartment building. Three men in plain clothes entered. A few minutes later they reappeared with José and shoved him into the back seat.

Two days later Jorge and Teresa read in the newspaper that Andres Nin, the POUM leader, had disappeared. It was rumoured that he had been tortured to death in prison by Soviet agents. In a city beset with rumours — *tomorrow there will be bread, the war will soon be settled* — one learned to tell which were real and which were false.

In a single day they had lost both a war and a revolution.

§

Late that night, Teresa, to the steady susurrus of Jorge's sleep, wrote a letter to Sandro. Everyone had suffered so much and yet they would suffer still more. She saw it clearly. They had been such fools, such innocents, such idealists, and to have it all come to this.

Again she burned the letter at the window and watched the smoke twirl toward the impassive stars.

§

The sound of Sandro scraping the wooden match across the side of the box filled the cavern. He was trying to remember a single line from Dante's *Paradiso* … From out of nowhere, a rush of energy, a "wind of light" roared up and through him, pouring out his chest. Lightning, not out of heaven, but up from the earth. *Is this what the mystics experienced in their ecstasies?* But it was beyond religion, had nothing to do with belief. Heat at his fingertips, the match now a twisted corpse, he leaned forward and lit the lamp.

§

In the dark kitchen, his father sat on a hard straight-backed chair, head bowed, hands clasping knees, waiting.

"Papa."

"I knew you would come, Sandro."

"Papa, what is it?"

"Pedro is dead."

Sandro gaped at his father. "What? Dead?" He collapsed into a chair across the table.

"The Cruzado brothers came today. They told us he was killed trying to escape. Shot in the back ... in the back ..."

Sandro stared at the table. "This ... I ... I should have tried to find him. Oh, God."

"No." The old man paused. "They asked where you were. We told them again the Reds had taken you." He swallowed heavily. "Emilio hit your mama in the mouth with his rifle butt. Alfonso knocked me to the ground when I tried to help."

There were three teeth on the table.

"Where is Mama?"

"Resting. She will be all right. We told them nothing, but they are angry with us. Many of the young people here have left to fight for the Reds and the anarchists, but they are losing. Few fight for the fascists. There are only old people and children left in the village. I fear the Falange will do something terrible to punish Arcasella. Even as boys, the Cruzados were cruel as wild dogs. *Salvajes*."

"Oh, God, Pedro, Pedro ..." Sandro looked up.

The old man didn't seem to hear.

§

The surface of the sea writhed in endless, restless fever, but beneath the churning waves, the deep maintained its eternal calm.

Sandro stared out at it from a clutter of bushes near the beach, hidden in the after-midnight darkness. His breath moved in and out with the waves. He wanted nothing more than to feel the cool, refreshing air on his skin. To rest, awake.

His father had told him that the war raged on, as he feared. He had no idea how long he had been living in the cave. Anger flowed through him like a charge of electricity, elemental, thick with energy.

One by one the villages and towns had fallen to the relentless approach of the fascists. The city of Gijón up the coast was bombarded and quickly surrendered. News of reprisals against villagers and townspeople came every day, old men and young, women and children, murdered against stone walls, as if the fascists wanted to root out a strain of bad seed.

Agustín said there were no details of Pedro's death, merely a report that he had been shot trying to desert. They didn't know where his body was buried.

At last, after all that has happened, I am forced to take sides.

§

Emilio and Alfonso Cruzado sat across from each other high in the loft of the abandoned barn. Hay and bits of grain were scattered on the rough wooden floor and stuck to their worsted pants. Emilio held a rifle in his lap, his nervous eyes flashing as he scanned the poplar-lined road leading into Arcasella, the houses on the edge of town and, beyond, the metallic blue sea. Emilio was thin and small and charged with a nervous, unpredictable energy. He smoked a bent cigarette.

Alfonso rubbed a revolver with an oily rag, the pistol disappearing in the maw of his thick, white hands. His eyes had the dull look of an overworked horse and his large sloping shoulders were hunched. He chewed on his lower lip.

"Where is he? He's late."

"How am I supposed to know? He said he'd be here just after dawn."

Alfonso turned to spit. As a swallow swept in and out of holes in the barn roof, he took aim at it.

From his hiding place under a deep pile of hay on the floor below, Sandro overheard their conversation. Next to him lay the bicycle he had stashed in the barn months before. He smelled a strange scent of lime and blood and hay dust.

Alfonso and Emilio rose at the sound of someone entering below. "There he is."

Emilio shushed his brother and turned his rifle toward the sound. Alfonso dumbly raised his pistol and pointed in the same direction.

Jesús Díaz leaped up the ladder and stuck his head into the loft. He nodded, hoisted himself up and sat next to Emilio in the hay.

"Anyone see you?" said Emilio.

"No."

Alfonso leaned over. "Did you bring us the map?"

Díaz reached into his inside jacket pocket and pulled out a piece of paper.

Emilio examined it. "*Cuándo?*"

"Monday, at five in the afternoon. My troops, about thirty of us, will come along this path," he pointed at the map, "and sweep into the village, here. We will first come to the square in front of the church. From there we will send out patrols to bring everyone in the village to the square. Then we will march them to the cemetery. You said there will be forty to fifty?" He asked Emilio.

"Give or take a handful."

"Do you expect any resistance?"

"None. No one here but old people, children, dogs."

"I don't know. It sounds too easy." Jesús Díaz leaned toward the window and glanced out. "None of the men have drifted back from the fighting at Gijón?"

"We have been watching day and night."

"I want you to keep watching. Get word to us if you see any men returning from there, Oviedo or the mountains." Díaz stood to leave.

After he left, the Cruzado brothers lingered for a few minutes.

"We will finally punish this village for its resistance," Emilio said.

"We will shoot them all?"

"Yes, even their skinny goats and dogs."

Alfonso and Emilio descended the ladder and turned to exit.

"Wait. What's that?" Emilio pointed at a pile of hay at one end of the barn.

Alfonso stood with his hand on the barn door and stopped at his brother's command.

Emilio yanked on the end of the curved handlebar. "What is this doing here?"

Alfonso shrugged. "So what? A bicycle. I am hungry for breakfast. *Vamos.*"

"Shut up!" Emilio stood the bicycle up and stared at it. "Whose house is nearby? Who would want to hide a bicycle in such a place?"

"It could be anyone's."

"*Sí,* of course, it could be, but I have my suspicions. Old man Agustín is a poor liar."

"Let's take it."

"No. We'll leave it here so no one is the wiser."

He let the bike fall and covered it again, taking handfuls of hay from a spot near Sandro's head.

Minutes later, fearful of the full daylight, Sandro set out across the field and made it back to the cave without incident. In a short while he had a heavy burlap sack packed and ready to go.

§

The soldiers, rifles raised, walked warily into the village square, Jesús Díaz, Emilio and Alfonso in the lead.

"I don't like it." Díaz, a pistol in his hand, stopped and surveyed the plaza. "Deserted. We will wait here until the patrols return."

At the edge of the square, across from the tall stone church, a café table and chairs had been set in the shade of an oak tree. Díaz and the Cruzado brothers sat down at the table while the soldiers lounged about on the ground in the only shade available. Two soldiers broke down the door of the locked café and came out moments later with carafes of water and several bottles of wine. Díaz dumped water in his left hand and wiped his slick leathery face with it, took a slug of wine from the bottle and passed it to Emilio.

As they waited, patrols of three or four men returned empty-handed from various parts of the village, reporting that they had seen and heard no one.

"How did they know we were coming?" Díaz accused Emilio. "Only you and your brother had knowledge of our plans. Perhaps we should take you two out to the cemetery. Yes, that is what we will do. You have wasted my time, both of you."

"We told no one," blathered Alfonso, shaking his head. "No one."

"Don't be a fool," Emilio hissed at Díaz. "Shoot him," he pointed at his brother, "but do not question my allegiance."

Finally, the last patrol returned. They, too, had nothing to report, except that all the boats in the harbour were missing.

From his hiding place atop the bell tower in the church across the square, Sandro watched the *capitán* drink. He watched as Emilio rose from his chair, shouting. Watched the *capitán* slam the bottle down on the table, draw his pistol and motion for Emilio to sit down. Sandro had his hand on the detonator handle, wondering if he had buried enough dynamite beneath the cobbles under the café table and chairs.

Emilio, still sitting, turned away from the *capitán* and shouted to Alfonso. The *capitán* calmly held the pistol at arm's length. The shot knocked Emilio out of his chair and onto the ground. The *capitán* stood, walked over to Emilio's body and kicked it. He turned toward Alfonso, who was crawling backward, trying to skitter away. The *capitán* strode over and put a single bullet into Alfonso's chest, the crack echoing off the walls of the square. Alfonso, on his back, spasmed once, twice, then lay still. Sandro leaned a little on the cold metal handle.

Something caught his attention. A young soldier, a boy who reminded him of Pedro, was crying, unaccustomed to the bloodletting. The *capitán* stood and stared at the young soldier. The *capitán* shouted, "Shut him up!" The boy put his head between his knees and wrapped his arms around it, trying to stifle his sobs. The *capitán* walked back to the table and drank from the bottle of wine, then motioned for his men to stand. With the *capitán* in the lead, the soldiers walked out of the square, glancing at the bodies of Emilio and Alfonso as they passed.

Sandro stayed in the bell tower until long after the column of soldiers had disappeared and night had come, covering the two inert bodies in the square with a blanket of darkness.

Out at sea, Agustín and Mercedes and the other villagers, in a cluster of fishing boats rocking on the waves, heard the church bells and Sandro's mother made the sign of the cross. The small flotilla of fishing craft turned about and headed to shore.

Later, under the oak tree, the villagers found the Cruzado brothers. They buried them as quickly as possible and scrubbed the square clean of the blood stains.

An hour after ringing the bells, Sandro was back in the cave. He paused, his brush in hand, and bowed his head to the booming silence.

§

A few weeks later, when Sandro entered his parents' house, his father came into the kitchen dressed in his nightshirt. The light of the candle he held revealed his sorrow. "My son. It is over. Franco and his fascists have won."

"When?"

"Three days ago."

"I see." Sandro sat down and said nothing.

§

Sandro sucked white pigment from a seashell into a hollow reed. Placing his left hand flat on the wall, he raised the reed and blew the pigment around his hand and splayed fingers.

He spent the rest of the day cleaning up, removing all signs of his presence. He burnt the wooden crates deep in the forest and packed supplies and tools to take back to his father's house. The cave looked ancient, empty, abandoned. Any lingering traces — recent smoke stains, footprints — could be attributed to the roving gypsies who passed through these regions from time to time and took shelter in local caves.

Sandro walked slowly to the cave mouth, stepped out into full daylight and looked up at the sky.

§

"When the gods descend as vultures, the city will burn. They will not be appeased until only bones and dust remain." The old gypsy held Jorge's hand lightly in her own, squinting at his palm.

Walking down the Ramblas late at night, keeping to the shadows, he had seen the gypsy woman seated on a blanket under a tree. "Your fortune?" she had croaked at him.

Tossing a coin in the gypsy's lap, he knelt down before her and offered his right hand.

All the hag wanted to talk about was the war. The fascists were drawing near — Franco's troops were perhaps a week away from Barcelona although Madrid was still holding out. It was clear to everyone except the most diehard militants that the Left had lost, the Republic had lost, the Revolution was dead, the end of the war not far off. Bombs had been dropped on the city intermittently for months, by the Italians, by the Germans, by the many enemies of Barcelona and Catalonia. Heaps of rubble were everywhere.

Jorge asked, "Will we ever achieve our Revolution?"

She waved her hand, dismissing his interest. "At a time like this, who cares?"

§

Jorge cut through an alley where the pavement was ankle-deep in shattered glass from nearby buildings. Over the past month, tens of thousands of people had left Barcelona and headed for the French border — walking, driving mule carts, in trucks and cars. He and Teresa planned to leave themselves in the next day or two.

When he returned to the apartment, Teresa, standing at the window, tossed him a half-hearted greeting. Jorge took a chair at the kitchen table and picked up a well-thumbed newspaper.

"City feels deserted. Probably half empty already."

"Hmm." Teresa did not turn from the window.

Jorge feigned interest in what he was reading.

"Look what I found." She handed him several pieces of clothing. "A woman I know gave me these today." She held out two heavy wool sweaters, one blue, one grey. "They belonged to her husband."

"What happened to him?"

"Killed at the front last summer." She held out the blue sweater. "One is for you."

"A good sweater. But yours will be much too big."

"No, it's perfect — I'll be able to wear another underneath."

"Tomorrow?"

"Yes. It's time."

§

By early morning they were on the road outside Barcelona, heading for the French border. A line of families, soldiers, vehicles, men on horses and a few on bicycles streamed both ahead and behind. The fields looked grey and defeated, the trees black sentinels against the sky. Jorge toted a worn suitcase; Teresa hauled a large canvas packsack stuffed with clothing and food.

The driver of an old truck honked as he passed, stopped and leaned out. "I almost didn't recognize you."

"Luis! You have a truck! Where did you get it?" He was a fellow member of POUM.

"Don't ask. But hop on, I may have enough petrol to get us to the border"

The back of the open truck was filled with a motley assortment of men, women and children. One boy had a bandage across his head. Sandro and Teresa squeezed on, their legs dangling off the back, and the truck inched forward, moving slowly along the roadway crowded with refugees.

Two hours later, Teresa banged the side of the truck, shouting, "Stop! Stop!" The truck ground to a halt. Teresa leaped off and ran back down the line, looking at faces. She stopped. "Adam?"

His face shaded with three days of growth, he looked at her blankly, then brightened. "Teresa? Yes, yes, Adam Weatherhead at your service." He saluted and smiled.

"Come with me." They hurried back to the truck and climbed aboard.

Jorge and Adam shook hands. "You look like you've been through hell," Jorge said.

"Yes, well, I guess I have been. When the International Brigade left, I signed up to return to the front. I just got back a week ago from the battle at the Ebro. We've lost it all, haven't we?"

"I'm afraid it is true." Teresa nodded.

"I guess we are headed to the French refugee camps."

Jorge nodded. "There is no choice. We must leave. Franco's Nationalists are showing no mercy."

There was a long silence as the truck chugged up a hill.

Teresa sat between them, staring at the ground passing between her feet. "I must tell you both, I will not stay long in France. As soon as it is possible to leave the camp, I will find my way, somehow, across the south of France to the sea where I can find a fishing boat going to Gijon. I have made up my mind."

Jorge blurted out, "You are going to try to find Sandro! I will come, too. A woman cannot do it alone."

"No, I have thought about this, Jorge. I will go alone. The woman who gave us the sweaters was well off. She also gave me a little money. She has been very kind."

Adam looked at her. "You are either a very brave or a very foolish woman. I wish you luck."

"I have been planning it for months, talking to people who know the way."

When they neared the border, everyone clambered out and joined the crowds trudging along the roadway.

"I will go with you when you leave the camp." Jorge lifted his suitcase.

"No. It is not necessary, Jorge. I will be fine. I know where to find him."

Adam, too, wanted to help her, but his health was nearly ruined from his time at the front. He knew it was impossible. She would have refused, anyway. "Have you heard from him?" he asked.

Teresa tilted her head to look at him. "No."

§

Sandro, blinking, stepped into the house. Daylight bothered his eyes and he was glad to come into the cool interior where light fell in bands across the stone floor.

His eyes scanned the table for a letter. Nothing. He had had no response to the two letters he had sent her since emerging from the cave. He wondered if he should leave immediately for Barcelona. It would still be dangerous, especially for one who did not have certain proof that he had fought on the side of the fascists. Also, he had no money. The long period as a hermit had altered him. He could not bear to be with people. Strangers caused him distress. And yet, now that he was out of the cave, the war over, Teresa's voice and face once again returned to him. She was luring him gently back into the world.

Slowly, over a month, two months, he re-established a life with the other villagers. He let it be known that he had spent the war fighting for Franco in the area around Teruel, but had lost his papers. Everyone "reinterpreted" what they had done during the war. Former communists proclaimed their allegiance to Franco, Hitler and Mussolini. Neighbours spoke out against neighbours. There was no mercy, only hate and calls for revenge.

Sandro spoke to as many returning soldiers as he could, interrogating them so that he might build a believable past. He learned enough from the experiences of others that he was able to convince the authorities that he had spent the war fighting for the "true Spain". And yet the interviewers, sent occasionally from Oviedo to search out former communists and leftists in the villages, never seemed entirely satisfied. Because he had been recognized at several roadblocks on his way back to Arcasella in the early days of the war, he feared someone might remember him. Proof would not be necessary; suspicions alone would be enough.

§

Sandro, hearing the door to the kitchen open, rose from his chair in the front room where he was reading a three-day-old newspaper from Oviedo. He thought it was his mother returning from the market in the village and he went out to greet her.

A figure stood in the blazing light of the back doorway, but it wasn't his mother.

"Sandro?"

Leaning on the back of a chair, he shook his head, unable to speak.

"Sandro? Is it you?"

"How ... how can this be?"

"I don't know. I've been traveling a long time. I left a refugee camp in France. I knew you would still be here. I ... I knew it. I am very thirsty." She set her dusty packsack down on the flagstones.

Sandro fumbled about, getting her water. He handed it to her unsteadily.

"You doubted I would come?" She took a long deep draft of water from the mug. He watched her head tilt back, took in the paleness of her throat.

When Sandro's mother came in, they were laughing and she knew without being told that this was the Teresa Sandro had mentioned.

§

Later, they walked by the sea in the warm spring dusk. "Your letters kept me alive. They saw me through the war. I had to burn them, but I remembered your words. I thought of you every day. I knew that everything would be possible when the madness was over."

"Is it really over?"

They sat in the sand, watching the waves break, low rollers reflecting the gold of the setting sun. As the sky slipped into deeper and deeper layers of indigo they leaned closer. Finally, in full darkness, all that remained were lines of white foam.

Mark Frutkin

Afterward, they lay shoulder to shoulder gazing at the stars.
"Three long years burned up in an instant."
"Time is meaningless. We have denied it."

§

All afternoon the sea burned white with August heat. The years had passed quickly. Sandro, alone in his father's fishing boat, was puttering back to the harbour, having caught two small fish in ten hours. Despite the poor take, he couldn't help but enjoy the view of Arcasella as he entered the bay. The village and beach curved between two headlands like a scimitar moon. He could see the road that led into the forest, where the cave entrance was hidden, and the river descending from foothills to flow under the bridge .

The wider European war had left them more or less untouched. Spain, already on its knees, was able to stay out of it because it could offer nothing. Its recovery from its own war was slow and difficult, in Arcasella as elsewhere. Sandro and Teresa scratched out a living, taking over the garden and the fishing boat from Sandro's parents as they grew older. But food was measured day by day in smaller and smaller amounts.

In 1941, Teresa bore a son. In 1943, another. Two more small mouths to feed, but Sandro was overjoyed. When Agustín died in the year after the birth of his first son, Sandro thought only of what his grandson would miss with his passing.

As he came in from the sea with the day's catch, Sandro gazed at the village. *Everything is the colour of dust.*

And then finally, after years of hardship, they heard the world war had ended. In Arcasella the celebrations were muted. At last it was over. "Now that Hitler and Mussolini are dead, Franco cannot last. The only fascist left in all of Europe. It's impossible."

§

Sandro decided it was time to "discover" the caves. He had been discussing it with Teresa for weeks.

He told the old priest, Padre Esteban, that he had found an important Paleolithic cave site. He informed the mayor, as well. Sandro explained patiently and soon both came to understand what the discovery could mean for the village. He wrote to several important newspapers announcing his find, knowing the discovery of the cave at Lascaux in France only a few years earlier was still fresh in people's minds.

A FIND AS IMPORTANT AS ALTAMIRA AND LASCAUX read the headline in the Oviedo newspaper. Reporters from Madrid, Barcelona and Paris came to Arcasella. Sandro, calling himself an amateur archaeologist and an avid cave explorer, was widely praised. Over the next few months, experts from around the world visited the town, followed by groups of archaeology students. Even a few well-heeled tourists began to make their way over the mountains or along the coast.

Arcasella, just as Sandro had foreseen, experienced newfound prosperity. A two-story hotel was constructed. Roads were improved. The first new bakery in over a century was built on the edge of the village. Even the notoriously skinny local dogs filled out.

Because Sandro had discovered the caves and had some knowledge of archaeology from his summer at Linares, the mayor appointed him the administrator of the site and offered him a small salary.

§

Sandro and Teresa stood outside their house looking up into the night sky. Over the sea a comet appeared and disappeared in the same moment. Inside the house, the boys were asleep, his old mother in another room nodding off in her chair, a rosary dangling from her left hand.

§

Through the tall windows of the government office, Sandro could see down to the harbour where a few fishing boats rocked in their berths and three old men sat mending nets, an orange cat at their feet. He had been interviewed in this room before, by *Señor* Gonzaga, the official from Oviedo who traveled to Arcasella every few months to repeat the same dull questions. "Where did you spend the war years? Tell me about the battle around Teruel? What was your division?" and Sandro replied with the same well-rehearsed answers, gleaned from talking to veterans in Oviedo and Gijón. Considering the inefficiency of the fascist bureaucracy and Gonzaga's fumbling, he had felt safe.

But this time was different. There was a second interviewer and Sandro did not like the look of him.

"This is *Señor* Moro from Madrid," Gonzaga said, introducing him. "He will be interviewing you when I have finished."

Señor Moro nodded, without saying a word. While Sandro, sitting in a chair in front of the wide desk, half-listened to Gonzaga's tired questions, he looked Moro over. He had shiny black hair and was dressed in an elegant grey suit. Sandro knew he was with the secret police, knew his questions would be more incisive than those of Gonzaga, knew that he would see through the holes in his story. The reprisals against the Left had been going on for years throughout Spain and would likely continue. *Señor* Moro's presence meant his fate had already been decided.

Moro himself, of course, wouldn't wield the truncheons in the prison cell, there would be others to do the dirty work. Sandro's first thought was of escape, but they would hold Teresa and his sons hostage to keep him from running. If he fled, his family would be ruined. He also knew any attempt to reach the French border was doomed; it was too far. A small boat, at night, maybe, but no, it was too dangerous for the children.

Gonzaga, bowing and grinning, relinquished his chair to *Señor* Moro, who smiled charmingly at Sandro as he sat down. "So, *Señor* Risco Cánovas, please tell me about your life during the war. I would ask you to include every detail."

By the time Sandro left the office two hours later, he knew he had only two days, maybe three, before they arrested him. From what he had heard about Franco's prisons, he knew he would not last long before the beatings, disease or lack of food killed him.

Sandro stood on the bridge in the heart of Arcasella. He paced, stopped, stared down at the water, turned, paced again. He gazed out at the persistent sea. There was no escape.

§

Later that afternoon, he walked down into the village to see Padre Esteban.

"Come in, my son." The old priest padded down the hall into his shadowy sitting room, Sandro following.

"Padre, I have come to ask a favour."

The old man sat, clasped his hands together and rested them on his belly. Bits of food stained the front of his loose black cassock. *A bit of egg yolk perhaps*, thought Sandro, who had always liked the old priest.

The padre smiled. "I would be more than happy, whatever it is. A man of my age can do so little in this world. I consider it my duty."

"Yes." Sandro pulled a letter from inside his shirt. "Would you hold on to this letter for one year? When the year is up, give it to Teresa. That is all I ask. Tell no one you have it, not even Teresa, but be sure to give it to her when the time has come. No matter how much you think it may comfort her in difficult times, she must not see it before then."

"That is all?"

"Yes, but it is *very* important, *extremely* important. I must have your word. Will you do it, Padre?"

"Of course, my son. I am old enough to know not to ask questions."

"I will tell you that I must go away for a while, but I hope to return in a year or two."

"It will be very difficult for Teresa and your sons, will it not?"

"Yes. But it will be much more difficult for them if I do not go."

"I see. As long as I am alive they will not suffer. I do not have much, but still I have more than I need. Your sons and your wife will not go hungry."

"I am grateful for your help."

Sandro stood to go. The old priest took Sandro's hand in both of his and nodded sadly. "You must do what you must do. Do not worry. Your secrets will be safe with me. God go with you, my son."

"And you, Padre, and you."

When Sandro had left, Padre Esteban took the letter next door to the empty church. He genuflected, made the sign of the cross and climbed the two stairs to the altar. Leaning across the white marble, he opened the door to the tabernacle and removed the pyx, the small silver vessel holding the sacred Hosts, placing it aside on the altar. Reaching into the tabernacle, he loosened its white silk lining, slipped in the letter and tucked the lining in again. He was satisfied the letter would be invisible even on close inspection. Bowing his head, he said a heartfelt prayer and left the church.

§

The next evening after dinner, Sandro kissed José and Fernando on the forehead and held them close. He turned to Teresa and said, "I am going fishing."

"Why? You don't normally fish at night."

"Perhaps the fishing will be better than by day." He gave her a long kiss, looked into her eyes and turned away.

Teresa stood in the doorway and watched him go.

"Sandro," she called.

He turned.

She waved.

He hesitated, waved back, then walked on.

Do not call me again or I will not have the strength to do this. He felt her gaze on the back of his neck. He tried not to think about what he was leaving. She did not call out to him again.

§

Sandro walked across the bridge to the deserted harbour in twilight, the sea calm. In a shed on the dock, he found what he was looking for, forgotten, upside down, in the rafters. Hauling down his father's small rowboat, he threw in the oars and a pile of oily rags from a corner of the shed and lugged it to the old fishing vessel in the harbour. He dropped the rowboat in the water and tied it to the stern of the larger boat, then threw the rags on the deck, its old wooden slats as grey as bad weather.

He backed out, turned and headed out to sea. Fifteen minutes later, Sandro cut the motor and drifted. No other boats crossed the bay. He took one last look at Arcasella.

Sandro moved cautiously, focusing on his hands, piling the oily rags on the deck, adding a few pieces of splintered wood. Into the rowboat he dropped a sack he brought with him from the house — bread, dried sausage, several skins of water, a knife, a fishing line and hooks.

Slipping a box of matches from his pocket, he removed one matchstick and struck it on the side of the boat. He held the flame to half a dozen of the rags before tossing it on the pile. Soon the fire had spread along an entire side of the vessel.

Stepping over the stern, Sandro swung down into the rowboat, untied the rope and took up the oars. He pulled hard half a dozen times and glided away from the fishing vessel, now engulfed in flames against the falling night. He imagined his father standing on the deck, as he had seen him so many times before.

Sandro began rowing in the direction of France, Arcasella dissolving in the darkness. *When Franco is gone, I will return. A year, perhaps two.*

§

Padre Esteban, celebrating the Mass, opened the tabernacle to remove the Hosts and remembered again about the letter. It was a Sunday, almost a year since Sandro's disappearance. It had been a year steeped in sorrow, but he had kept his word. No one had learned of the letter, even though the authorities had come to him and others in the village to ask questions about Sandro. They refused to believe that he was dead, either by suicide or accident.

The padre also refused to accept that Sandro had killed himself. He had seen him the day before the terrible event and he had not appeared to be a man intent on ending his life. Padre Esteban had tried to console Teresa, whom he would see from time to time in the village. Once, she had stopped him in the street and wept on his shoulder. He had almost shared Sandro's secret, but caught himself. He had given his word.

Teresa knew that the sacks of food that had appeared on her doorstep from time to time in the past year had come from the padre. Once she had seen his housekeeper trundling down the hill in the early-morning mist only to find at her feet the bag of potatoes the woman had left on the doorstep. Teresa knew the padre was trying to let her maintain her dignity in trying times and she secretly thanked him for it.

§

The priest was short of breath when he finished the Mass and headed back to the parish house. He instructed his housekeeper that he would take a rest in his room.

Several hours later the housekeeper knocked lightly on his door. When he did not respond, she knocked harder. Unsure what to do, she opened the door a crack and called to him. When he still did not respond, she eased the door open and saw him lying on his back in the bed, his mouth wide. *The old can slip away so easily, in a single unguarded moment.*

§

Late that Sunday, Teresa sat in a chair on her front porch. She bit her lower lip, thinking; she held Sandro's sketchbook in her lap. Before she opened the book, she saw the padre's housekeeper struggling up the lane in the failing light.

"Padre Esteban passed away this afternoon." The housekeeper explained that, unfortunately, she would no longer be able to bring sacks of food. They exchanged words of sadness and regret and the housekeeper returned the way she had come.

Teresa sighed, left the sketchbook unopened and watched the last light of day burn on the water.

A Man in Flames

July 1982

Adam Weatherhead had a full head of white hair, a voluminous white beard, full lips, penetrating green eyes and a commanding presence. Despite the Spanish heat, he wore a three-piece tweed suit in a style that was never out of fashion. He was 67, a retired Classics professor from the University of Toronto.

Adam sat on a train with Elizabeth, his wife. They were traveling over the Picos de Europa mountains from León to Oviedo where they would catch a bus for Arcasella, following in Sandro's footsteps.

"I just don't understand how he lasted so long."

Elizabeth looked up from her novel. "Who?"

"Franco."

Over the years, Adam had had no response to his letters addressed to "Sandro Risco Cánovas, Arcasella, Asturias, Spain." In fact, he had no way of knowing if Sandro had ever made it back to his home village at all.

During the war in Spain, Adam had seen things he would never forget. Yet he still longed for the place, its severe landscape, the sound of Spanish voices. He had always planned to return after the war, but feared arrest by the fascists. He had put his plans on hold, waiting for Franco's demise. He had heard about the terrible reprisals, the torture and murders in the prisons. Even after a liberalizing of fascist policies in the fifties and sixties, Adam was still not comfortable with the idea of returning.

Sitting on the train, he marveled that it had been forty-three years since he had walked out of Spain and into France. It had taken him the better part of a lifetime to get back.

The train began to climb, the grade rising slowly through sere countryside. The locomotive dragged the cars first into the foothills, then higher and higher into the mountains. Patches of snow glittered on distant peaks, sheer rock in every direction. Even the light looked hard.

Adam wondered what would be waiting in Arcasella. The fading memory of a friend long dead? A grizzled, barely recognizable face? Or simply an absence, a man erased entirely from history and memory.

Adam leaned back. The train dipped and climbed, sweeping in great curves around mountain bellies. They had come through the highest pass and were descending now. Elizabeth slept.

§

After a two-hour bus ride from Oviedo, in a blunt-nosed Mercedes that roared through rich green country, rolling foothills, and villages hanging above the sea, Adam and Elizabeth disembarked next to the trim harbour in Arcasella. The air smelled of saltwater.

They approached an old man in a cap, who was sitting in the shade mending a net. The dog sitting next to him rose to its feet and sniffed their shoes.

"*Señor, por favor*, I am looking for a man, an old friend — his name is Sandro Risco Cánovas. Do you know where I can find him?"

A puzzled look came to the fisherman's face. "I have not heard that name in many years." He pointed. "His son, *Don* Fernando, owns a hotel, over there. The Arcasella Playa, across the bridge." He went back to his mending.

Adam and Elizabeth picked up their bags and walked across the bridge. From there they could see steep wooded mountains on the inland side and, on the other, the river widening into an estuary that emptied into the nearby sea. There was little activity. The dog followed them halfway across the bridge, then returned.

Beyond the bridge, a number of small hotels lined a street parallel to the beach.

The Hotel Arcasella Playa appeared to be nothing more than a large house. Cascades of exotic red blossoms overflowed bulky earthenware pots on the front porch.

Elizabeth stopped to admire them. "I'd like to paint these."

Behind the desk, in the lobby cramped with furniture and overgrown rubber plants, sat a young woman. "*Buenos días*. You would like a room?" There was a hint of something in the girl's eyes, but Adam couldn't place it.

Adam nodded. "*Sí*."

They registered and handed over their passports. "Ah, Canada," said the young woman upon glancing at the covers. She held out a key.

"*Gracias*." Adam paused and the girl waited expectantly for him to speak. "One other thing. I am looking for someone, an old friend. I don't know if he's still here or not, but perhaps you could help me locate him."

"Yes? His name?"

"Sandro Risco Cánovas."

The girl gave him a blank look. "This is the name of my grandfather. But he has been gone for many years."

"Gone?"

"Yes." She hesitated. "He died soon after the war. Not our war, but the world war. How did you know him?"

"We were friends. Long ago. Just before the civil war started."

"I see. You should speak to my father. He is busy in the kitchen right now, but later, perhaps after dinner, you could meet with him?"

"Yes. Yes, I'd like that."

At the end of a hall on the first floor, Adam swung the door of their hotel room open. It was dark but for brilliant slats of light bleeding through the shutters. *Like lines in an illuminated manuscript.* Adam flung the shutters wide to the sea and a lemon-slice of beach arcing in a long sweep before them.

After a short rest they walked along a pathway behind the beach. Beyond the village the hills quickly rose into mountains, clouds of mist winding in tendrils among distant peaks.

That evening they had dinner in the restaurant of the twelve-room hotel. The short, hard-working proprietor, *Don* Fernando, and his wife Rosa, after running the hotel all day, cooked and waited on tables at night. Seven of the nine tables in the cool white-walled restaurant were occupied.

Don Fernando took their orders, left an open bottle of red wine from Valladolid on their table and hurried off to the kitchen.

After a meal of fresh hake, Adam asked *Don* Fernando if he could speak to him about a private matter. By his questioning look,

Adam suspected that his daughter had not yet told him about their connection.

Don Fernando looked around the restaurant. "*Sí*, of course. When the other guests have left, I will join you." Years of hard work in the hotel had left deep lines in his face. "What does it concern?"

"Many years ago, when I lived in Spain, I knew your father."

Don Fernando paused in silence, a dirty plate in each hand. He stared at Adam. "You knew *mi padre*?"

"I met him along the Camino Santiago. Before the war."

"I will be back shortly."

After the other guests left, *Don* Fernando returned with three brandy glasses upside down in one hand and a bottle in the other. He sat down.

"So how is it you knew my father?"

Adam related the story of the time he had spent in the beech tree with Sandro. *Don* Fernando listened, nodding every few moments. "I have a vague memory of my father telling this story about the tree. He told me, or perhaps my mother told me, when I was a young boy. I thought it was a fairy tale." He turned to look at Elizabeth. "And you, *Señora*, did you also know my father?"

"No. But Adam has told me much about him. I feel as if I knew him."

"Please forgive my being forward, but your daughter said Sandro died soon after the world war. Do you mind if I ask what happened?"

"I do not like talking about such things, but since you were a friend of my father's in those times I will tell you what I can recall. For many years everyone thought my father had fought at Teruel, but then, shortly before my mother died, she told me he had hidden during the war. He stayed in a cave, like a hermit. She did not tell me much, but she said it was very hard for him. Early in the war he had seen terrible things. He did not want to be involved. He thought it was madness. When the war ended, he came out and tried to live a normal life.

"The years after the civil war were hard. There was little food and much suffering. Soon after the world war ended, my father died in a fire on a boat out on the bay. Some said it was suicide because the secret police were looking for him, but I do not believe that. Others said it was an accident. My mama believed he hadn't died at all. But he never returned. She was left with two young boys — my brother José, who lives in Barcelona, and myself. My mama — her name was Teresa — died two years ago."

Adam paused on hearing the name. He took a fortifying drink of brandy.

"What happened, on the boat, I mean?"

"No one knows for sure. As I recall from stories, *mi padre* told Mama he was going fishing. He left in the early evening. My father was out in the bay. It was dusk. Some children on the beach spotted the burning boat and told the fishermen, but by the time they reached it Papa's boat had sunk. His body was never found. Mama seldom talked about it."

"I'm sorry."

"It was long ago."

There was an uncomfortable silence. Adam, Elizabeth and *Don* Fernando sipped their brandies.

Elizabeth looked at *Don* Fernando and decided a change of subject was in order. "I've heard there are famous caves near Arcasella. It is one of the reasons we have come here. I'm an artist, you see, and quite interested in the ancient cave paintings. Where are they? Can we walk to them?"

"You have heard of our caves? My father discovered them, right after the war."

"Sandro *found* them?" Elizabeth looked at Adam.

"Are they the same ones he hid in during the war?" Adam asked.

"I don't know. But the painted caves are nearby."

Elizabeth produced a tourist map and he gave them directions. Adam could tell he had done the same thing hundreds of times for other tourists, but he did it with pride nonetheless.

"My daughter will show you the way."

Don Fernando disappeared under a tiled archway and a moment later the young woman they had met earlier stood at their table, smiling. "Tomorrow I will show you the way to the caves. My name is María."

They made arrangements to meet at ten o'clock the next morning in the lobby of the hotel.

§

The sunlit road ran beside the river, then turned and curved up into the foothills. María and Elizabeth walked side by side, while Adam followed a few steps behind. Adam guessed she was about eighteen years old; he overheard her tell Elizabeth she would be going to university next year.

"And what will you study?"

"I am interested in archaeology, like my grandfather Sandro. He discovered the *cuevas*."

"How did this happen?" Adam asked, catching up.

"It was soon after the war, 1947, I think. My grandfather became famous. My father says he brought Arcasella into the modern world. Before the caves were found, this was a poor village like any other. It was even without electricity."

A few other tourists were waiting to enter the caves when Adam, Elizabeth and María arrived. Their guide was a thin, excitable man, neither young nor old, dressed in a dusty suit. He raised his nose in the air and led the party of eight into the cave, which was lit with fluorescent lamps.

The ceiling was almost ten metres high, and the meandering tunnel was at least as wide. They walked through the rock-strewn chambers, stalactites hanging from the ceiling, stalagmites like rough cones sticking up from the floor. In some places they joined and formed columns. The group walked in single file. No one spoke.

When they arrived at the spacious circular gallery at the end of the tunnel, its ceiling like a dome, the guide stood in the centre, aimed his flashlight and turned in a circle. "Observe," he said. The small group gazed at the walls and its display of animal life, random signs, dots and etched lines. Parts of the gallery had thick flutings, places where calcite had formed striations on the walls. In other places the flowstone had formed sweeping draperies and sheets. The tourists began murmuring among themselves, pointing out various details in the shadows. The guide, drawing the crowd with him, slid closer to the wall where a pair of animated horses overlapped each other. He aimed the flashlight at the image and cleared his throat. He paused when he saw Adam hanging back. "*Señor*," said the guide, motioning him over — he could not begin unless he had the undivided attention of everyone present. Adam did not look up, but continued gazing at the wall. "*Espera*," he said.

Adam felt his breath quicken. He drifted farther from the group and examined a herd of ibexes, striking and elegant. *There is a presence here.*

As the guide led the group from section to section, Adam peered at the beasts shifting in light and shadow. The bulls, configured in economic black lines, floated upon the irregular stone walls like heavy drifting clouds. The walls rippled with spotted hides. Adam thought he could smell their sweet, heavy breath in the air.

§

Adam stood at the hotel window. He loved the wild thrash of the sea, the wash of sound, the eternal repetition of its crash and foamy hiss.

"I had a dream," he said to Elizabeth, turning to look at her in bed. He was just able to make her out in the shadows. "I stood before a bridge engulfed in flames. I felt intense heat. I understood that I had to cross the bridge, but I was afraid. I didn't know what was on the other side. I had to move, I couldn't stay frozen in fear. I had to act. As I stepped onto the bridge, I awoke."

§

Adam, his white beard waving in the sea breeze, crossed the bridge. He was heading from the hotel to the village to have lunch. After lunch he would walk to the caves again. Elizabeth, who wanted to paint on the beach in the afternoon, decided to stay behind.

Adam stopped in the middle of the bridge and looked down the short stretch of river where it widened before entering the sea. The sky, wind-scoured, high and blue when he left the hotel, had changed and was shrouded in seaborne mist. He stared into the water. It was black, cold and quick on the surface, but deep underneath he spied a hidden brilliance. *Maybe that's what Sandro found there, at the bottom of the world.*

§

Elizabeth sat and painted under a beach umbrella. Something was worrying her. Each time she raised the brush, dabbed with a bulb of pink oil to touch up the herring gull high in the left corner, she was overcome by her thoughts and lowered the brush again. She put the brush down on the lip of the easel and drummed her fingers on her thigh.

Earlier, María had handed Elizabeth a sketchbook.

"I believe you and *Señor* Weatherhead might find this interesting. It was Grandfather's. I found it among my grandmother's things several months ago."

María said no more but turned and walked back to the hotel.

Elizabeth had stared at the sketchbook with its plain black cover. She heard the blur of a radio in the distance as she began turning the pages: sketches of animals, as well as notes. She recognized the bison, horses and ibexes, the floating bull and, exactly as she had seen it on the cave walls a few days earlier, a hand. No birds. She wondered why there were so few paintings of birds in the caves.

It appeared Sandro had assembled the illustrations from fragments. The slope of a haunch, a horse head, ibex horns, curving forward, sweeping back. And in the second half of the book, complete figures, as if he had been constructing them, building them up bit by bit. *Why would he copy them in parts?*

At the back of the sketchbook she had found a list:

hematite
manganese dioxide
red ochre
yellow ochre
limonite
white kaolin

The list sent her back to the front of the book. She checked inside the cover and found a date written above his name: "*junio 1935, Sandro Risco Cánovas.*" On a whim she flicked to the back cover and checked for a date there, as well: "*abril 1939,* Cueva Arcasella." The earth fell away and she brought her hand slowly to her mouth.

Oh, my God.

She looked again at the two dates, checking carefully to see that nothing had been erased. The script of the two entries matched. *He discovered the cave in 1947?*

Elizabeth picked up her brush from the easel and tried to paint. The feel of the implement in her hand as she smoothed out the oils helped to calm her. She worked for a long while, but she wasn't painting at all, she was looking through the canvas.

§

After a meandering walk through the cave, Adam stood alone in the midst of what the brochure called "The Great Hall." One crowd of tourists had left and he heard another approaching. Beasts swirled round the rough circular room: hump-backed bison melded into a dozen wild horses that flowed into a herd of ibexes, their heads held high, some floating upside down or sideways, elegantly overlapped.

He gazed for a long time at the walls, noted how each animal was constructed of calligraphy-like strokes drawn without hesitation and with a purity of vision.

§

That evening Elizabeth and Adam ate again in the hotel's restaurant, white walls accented with doorframes of dark wood. Toward the end of the meal, *Don* Fernando came to their table with an open bottle of wine, a fulsome Rioja, and filled their glasses.

"And how were the caves today, *Profesor*? I have noticed you go often. Why is that?"

"I find them fascinating."

"Are you looking for something?"

Adam tilted his head, puzzled. "No, not really. But I did want to ask you, *Don* Fernando, what was it like here, in Arcasella, before your father found the caves?"

"I was a very young boy, so I do not remember it well. But my mother would tell me about it. She said the discovery of the *cuevas* was the most important thing that ever happened in Arcasella. Before that, we were just a small fishing village. No tourists came here."

"Do you like all these people coming to your village now?" Elizabeth asked.

Fernando shrugged. "*Sí*. It is my life. If people did not come to see the caves, there would be no reason for this hotel, this restaurant. There are many places with better beaches. Without the hotel, I would be a fisherman. There are not so many fish any more. Some days the men return after twelve, eighteen hours with empty nets. It is a hard living. I, too, have worked hard all my life, and my wife. And now my daughter. But the caves will not go away. Unlike the fish, the caves will stay, and people will come to look at them. It is a good life."

"Did your father grow rich with the discovery?"

"No, no, not at all, *Señora*. When he announced that he had discovered the caves, the town asked him to manage them. The people here gained many jobs from the *cuevas*. He was a kind man, a generous man, my father. *Muy generoso*."

"I'm sorry I was not able to see him again. It would have been a great honour," Adam said.

"I think my father would also have been honoured, *Señor* Weatherhead. There was no one he did not get along with. Well, almost no one."

"Oh? He had enemies?"

"During the war, it was impossible not to have enemies. My father and grandfather refused to take sides, so they were hated by both Right and Left. But it was long ago."

Fernando pushed the cork back into the bottle and walked to the kitchen.

§

The next day, when the cave was closed to the public for siesta, Adam again entered, having been ushered through the locked wooden door by the head administrator, *Señor* López. Adam had explained that he was a professor and was conducting a study of the caves.

After a twenty-minute walk, they came again to the great hall. Adam turned full circle in admiration.

"Some of the other famous caves have works on the ceilings." *Señor* Lopez explained. "Altamira, Lascaux, others, too."

Adam stared. From a cleft in the wall it appeared the animals poured out in both directions. "What's that? There's something in the ibex herd there, deep inside the cleft, something standing up."

Señor Lopez aimed his flashlight. *"Ay, sí* — the experts say he is a *mago*, dressed in the skin of a bison. See the hump, the shoulders, the large head? You know this word, *mago*?"

"*Mago, mago*? Ah, I see. A shaman." Adam paused. "I think he's in flames. From this angle that's what it looks like. I don't think he's dressed in a bison skin at all — those are flames leaping up around him."

Señor Lopez gazed intently at the image. "I think you are correct, *Profesor*. *Sí*. A man in flames."

§

Elizabeth stared into her cup of espresso. Adam had already left to attend a Saturday choral concert at the church.

Twenty minutes later, she entered the cave with a crowd of Spanish families, English, French and German tourists, about thirty in all, guided by a stocky college girl in a green uniform.

As they walked, the guide politely answered questions from the tourists and held the hand of a little boy. Elizabeth was surprised again at how long it took to walk the sinuous caverns to the painted rotunda at the end. In the great hall the young woman began to lecture on several of the painted beasts, the crowd moving along with her from ibex to horse to bison.

As they stood before a particularly voluptuous painting of a deer, Elizabeth looked with a painter's eye. *What grace. Transcendent, yet entirely realistic. They're ... what is it? "Preternatural."*

The overhead lights flickered, off and on, off and on, then went out for good.

The guide clicked on her flashlight, its light surprisingly weak, and told the crowd not to worry but to follow her in single file out of the cave. She took two steps, turned to make sure the crowd was following, stumbled on a rock and dropped the flashlight. Elizabeth could hear the girl scrabbling in the dark and the distinct *click-click, click-click* once she had found it. Nothing. The flashlight was dead.

The tourists began to panic, a few children whimpered for their mothers and the guide told everyone in a loud, strict voice to sit down. She said it in Spanish first, followed by English and German. Elizabeth tried to see her hand before her face and couldn't. Someone lit a match. It burned out instantly. People whispered or spoke for a few moments, then stopped, as if their conversations had been extinguished, overwhelmed by the darkness.

Elizabeth had never experienced a silence like this. The blackness was total, thick, textured.

Suddenly, the images surrounding her reappeared in her mind, as if painted on the inside of her skull. Sandro had placed the beasts in strange arrangements, positioned in relation to bulges in the stone (one lump in the wall depicted the hump of a bison), but free for the most part of traditional concepts of order. *He must have had to learn to lose his balance, to forget up from down so the beasts could float. A kind of dying. He must have literally lost track, lost his mind.*

The lights came on full force without warning. Elizabeth found herself closer to the wall than she had expected. She was next to the tracing of a white hand hidden among a group of wild horses. She had needed to go deeper into the dark, like Sandro, before it would speak to her.

§

When she walked into the hotel room Adam was sitting up in bed, reading, his shoes neatly side by side on the floor. He spoke without looking up. "I couldn't find you on the beach. Painting not going well?"

Elizabeth bit her lip and walked to the window. "I went to the caves."

Adam looked up. "Really? What prompted that?"

"Adam, this is difficult to say, so I might as well say it right out. He didn't *discover* them, he *painted* them. Sandro. He painted the cave, while he was hiding there during the war."

Adam turned his head and stared at her. "What? I don't believe it. Wasn't the cave authenticated by scientists, experts?"

"María gave me an old sketchbook of Sandro's. I've been questioning her. As you know, she has an interest in archaeology and is extremely well-informed about the caves. She reminded me that it's very difficult to determine the age of a cave painting. Radiocarbon testing is almost useless. For wall paintings, I mean, especially if no organic material is used in the pigment. If it's all mineral, there's no irrefutable way to date them. The sculpted objects found on the floor of a cave are easier to date, apparently on the basis of already known artistic styles. I suspect Sandro brought some sculptures, and perhaps some charcoal, from another, genuine cave — probably the one where he worked that summer. Then he 'discovered' them buried in the Arcasella cave and used them as proof."

"But it would be an enormous project. It would take so long."

"I suspect these were the caves where he hid for the duration of the war — it would be time enough."

"But why? Why would he do it?"

"I don't know. Why does anyone make art? The creative inhabits a body and forces its way out. Maybe he did it for the village, for his people. It put Arcasella on the map. For the first time, people here prospered. I suspect Sandro had planned it for a long time. Hiding from his enemies during the war became an excuse to disappear."

"This sketchbook you mentioned. Do you still have it?"

"Yes. María said she didn't want it back. She gave it to me."

"Could it be a fake? Easier to fake a document than a cave full of paintings."

"No. There was no reason for Sandro to fake a sketchbook — and every reason to fake the paintings."

Elizabeth reached inside her bag and pulled out the sketchbook. Adam paged through it and recognized the illustrations. "By God, he had a fluid hand."

"Look at the dates, Adam, at the beginning and the end."

Adam glanced inside the front and back covers and slowly closed the sketchbook.

§

Placing his pen on the desk, Adam stood, threw open the shutters and let a flood of light into the room. The sea, sparkling, crashed against the shore. It was the morning of their last day in Arcasella.

"It suddenly hit me, Elizabeth. I'm an old man. When I leave a place, any place, I don't know if I'll ever see it again, don't know if I'll return." He looked at her, sensing she was listening now. "You'll have me cremated, won't you? I'd like to be cremated."

"Oh, don't be ridiculous." She picked up her novel and returned to reading.

A short while later, in the early-morning mix of sea-mist and sunlight, Adam walked alone along the beach. Suddenly, two young boys, seven or eight years of age, lit out of the tall grass and across the strand to the water's edge. Even from a distance Adam could tell they were excited about something. The boys had found an old bicycle, its rear wheel half buried in sand, seaweed hanging in strips from the handlebars and spokes. The boys were digging it out with cupped hands. With little trouble they freed it, stood it up and proudly wheeled it away.

§

Suck the marrow of the world out of a burned bone and spit in patterns on the wall, naming beasts, whispering their secrets of death and fertility. Bring thunder into the moment and stir life with a stick of lightning.

As the day's dying light fell like fine cinnamon-coloured sand, Adam walked along the dirt road that ran from the beach to the cave, a net bag swinging from his left hand. Inside the bag were a flashlight, Sandro's sketchbook, a few dry sticks and matches.

Before dinner, Adam had explained to Elizabeth that he wanted to make one last visit to the caves before they left in the morning. He had arranged with *Señor* Lopez to meet him at the cave entrance that evening, after the cave had closed to the public.

As Adam walked along the road, scruffy weeds growing at its edges, he saw *Señor* Lopez waiting for him. He unlocked the heavy wooden door leading to the cave. "You have a *linterna*, *Señor* Weatherhead? The electric lights, they are turned off for the night."

Adam nodded and raised the bag in his hand.

"Please, you will be careful?"

"Of course."

Adam walked along the familiar path, pointing the flashlight now at his feet, now ahead into the dark. A few bats swept by, quick arcs across his straight beam. When he arrived at the hall he stood in the centre and traced the backs of the beasts with his flashlight, its beam sliding over their curves, the light an impossibly delicate touch. He caressed their horns and flanks, as if redrawing them, tracing every line from mouth to tail to hoof, arched backs to soft bellies.

"Good evening, *Señor* Weatherhead."

Adam snapped his light in the direction of the voice.

"It's you."

"You do not seem surprised to see me."

"No. I figure you must know this cave better than anyone."

"Yes, it is true. I have spent many days here."

María stepped fully into the light. She was dressed in jeans, a red windbreaker and running shoes.

"Do you mind if I sit?"

They sat on flat stones across from each other, the net bag between them.

María looked around. "I love the feel of this place."

"I believe I know why you are drawn to it."

"And why is that?"

He didn't answer, but glanced at the bag between them. "I have the sketchbook you gave my wife."

"Ah, yes. Eventually, I am sure the truth will come out. Professionals will devise new tests, more precise measurements. The scientists are endlessly clever."

Adam nodded in agreement. "But, in the end, you and I know it doesn't matter. Look at that bull." He pointed the flashlight. "He is sad and sweet. Poor beast, I feel for him. His mouth is soft and wet, he thinks mostly of his belly. He is much like us."

María turned and they stared at the bull. *The spaces here, the silence, utterly empty, an abyss that yawns open forever.*

María turned back to him. "What happened to him here?"

"I have spent days in this cave trying to understand that. What happened? He saw the world had gone mad and there was nowhere for him to turn. He must have gone inside — inside the earth, inside himself."

"And what did he find there?"

"Only he could answer that."

She paused. "No, Professor, you are wrong — we *do* know what he found there. He is still alive. Alive in these paintings. Alive in this silence." María stared at the net bag at their feet.

Adam laughed lightly. "Along with the sketchbook, I have brought some dry sticks. Matches."

"You have come to burn it."

"Yes."

Adam emptied the bag onto the dirt floor, picked up the sketchbook and folded it open. He tore out a page with a bull's head on it, lit a match and held it at one corner. As it curled into flame, he placed the sheet under the dry sticks. He tore the pages and added them one by one, the animals on the walls awaking in the shimmering light.

The fire pulsed calm and steady. It would burn for a long time. Adam watched it glow in María's face as she gazed into its slow ascent.

Acknowledgements

Special thanks to Joy Gugeler, my hard-working editor at Raincoast, as well as Richard Taylor and Nicola Vulpe for their extremely generous editorial assistance and suggestions. Thanks to Michael Robinson for sending hard-to-find books my way and to Shawn Murphy for early research tips. And, as always, thanks to Elliot for asking and Faith for her perspective and discerning eye.

Other books in the Raincoast Fiction Imprint:

After Battersea Park by **Jonathan Bennett**
1–55192–408–0 $21.95 CDN $16.95 US
In a twist on the twins-separated-at-birth story Australian–Canadian
Jonathan Bennett pens a tale of 27-year-old brothers drawn toward a
reunion when a suicide note reveals the identity of their true parents.
In a chase that spans three continents, the estranged sons unravel the
wrenching events of London's Battersea Park twenty-three years earlier.

Finnie Walsh by **Steven Galloway**
1-55192-372-6 $21.95 CDN $16.95 US
Finnie Walsh is Paul Woodward's best friend, a hockey fanatic and the
tragic figure at the heart of a series of bizarre accidents that alter the
lives of the Woodward family in a comic tale of family, friendship,
redemption and legend.

Hotel Paradiso by **Gregor Robinson**
1–55192–358–0 $21.95 CDN $16.95 US
Journey Prize nominee Gregor Robinson's debut novel charts a season in
the life of a thirty-something expat banker in the Bahamian out-port of
Pigeon Cay. He has come to the subtropics in search of exotic escape,
but instead stumbles upon genteel corruption, white collar crime, racism
and murder.

Kingdom of Monkeys by **Adam Lewis Schroeder**
1–55192–404–8 $19.95 CDN $15.95 US
Charting the steamy jungles and murky depths of the South Seas,
Schroeder's collection cunningly exposes the vestiges of colonial power
in Asia, reinventing the exotic, the exquisite and the exiled while sinking
into a culture luxurious in irony and intrigue.

Rhymes with Useless by **Terence Young**
1-55192-354-8 $18.95 CDN $14.95 US
In a collection praised by *The Village Voice, Publisher's Weekly, National
Post* and the *Globe & Mail* Governor General's nominee Terence Young
creates both a litany of human foibles and its sensible antidote; regret
and forgiveness, suppressed desire and unleashed lust, dislocation and
homecoming.

Song of Ascent by **Gabriella Goliger**
1-55192-374-2 $18.95 CDN $14.95 US
Journey Prize winner Gabriella Goliger's finely-honed stories recount the
troubled lives of the Birnbaum family, displaced German Jews who flee
Hitler but cannot escape the shadow of the Holocaust. Their uprooted
existence takes them from Europe to the Holy Land to Montreal to relate
a history that explores the tense dialogue between present and past.